D0087285

The Canyons of Grace

With respect and
good wishes

Levi S. Peterson

ILLINOIS SHORT FICTION

Crossings by Stephen Minot
A Season for Unnatural Causes by Philip F. O'Connor
Curving Road by John Stewart
Such Waltzing Was Not Easy by Gordon Weaver

Rolling All the Time by James Ballard
Love in the Winter by Daniel Curley
To Byzantium by Andrew Fetler
Small Moments by Nancy Huddleston Packer

One More River by Lester Goldberg
The Tennis Player by Kent Nelson
A Horse of Another Color by Carolyn Osborn
The Pleasures of Manhood by Robley Wilson, Jr.

The New World by Russell Banks
The Actes and Monuments by John William Corrington
Virginia Reels by William Hoffman
Up Where I Used to Live by Max Schott

The Return of Service by Jonathan Baumbach
On the Edge of the Desert by Gladys Swan
Surviving Adverse Seasons by Barry Targan
The Gasoline Wars by Jean Thompson

Desirable Aliens by John Bovey
Naming Things by H. E. Francis
Transports and Disgraces by Robert Henson
The Calling by Mary Gray Hughes

Into the Wind by Robert Henderson
Breaking and Entering by Peter Makuck
The Four Corners of the House by Abraham Rothberg
Ladies Who Knit for a Living by Anthony E. Stockanes

Pastorale by Susan Engberg
Home Fires by David Long
The Canyons of Grace by Levi S. Peterson
Babaru by B. Wongar

THE CANYONS OF GRACE

Stories by
Levi S. Peterson

UNIVERSITY OF ILLINOIS PRESS

Urbana   Chicago   London

*Publication of this work was supported in part
by grants from the National Endowment for the Arts
and the Illinois Arts Council, a state agency.*

© 1982 by Levi S. Peterson
Manufactured in the United States of America

"The Confessions of Augustine," *Denver Quarterly* 12, no. 4
(Winter 1978).

"Trinity," *Ascent* 7, no. 1 (Fall 1981).

"Road to Damascus," *Dialogue: A Journal of Mormon Thought*
11, no. 4 (Winter 1978).

"The Shriveprice," *Sunstone* 6, no. 5 (September-October 1981).

"The Canyons of Grace," *Ascent* 7, no. 3 (Spring 1982).

Library of Congress Cataloging in Publication Data

Peterson, Levi S., 1933-
   The canyons of grace: stories.

   (Illinois short fiction)
   Contents: The Confessions of Augustine—Trinity—
Road to Damascus—[etc.]
   I. Title. II. Series.
PS3566.E73C3   813' .54   82-4720
ISBN 0-252-00997-5 (cloth)   AACR2
ISBN 0-252-00998-3 (paper)

SHIPPED AS PAPERBACK

To Althea and Karrin

Contents

The Confessions of Augustine

Augustine was converted beneath a fig tree. I was converted, if you allow a metaphoric extension, beneath a pine. For both of us there was also a pear tree.

My name is Fremont Dunham. I am forty-two, I live in Salt Lake City, I own a hardware store and lumberyard, and I am a Mormon. About a month ago my driver brought back from a remodeling job two boxes of books and papers. I found in one of the boxes a copy of the *Confessions* of Augustine. It sits on my desk among whole-sale quotations and manuals for the grading of lumber. It is an incongruity, perhaps even a perversity, that I take pleasure in this book, because like most Mormons I have believed that very little of importance happened to Christianity between the death of the last ancient apostle and the restoration of the Gospel through the prophet Joseph Smith.

Augustine's father was a pagan and his mother was a Christian. Augustine's mother could not command him to become a Christian, but her fervent desire followed him. He resisted his conversion and it came to him painfully. Afterward he wondered why he had fled from God for so long. He remembered a time when, as an adolescent, he had joined friends in the wanton destruction of fruit in a neighbor's pear tree. The act was not trivial and commonplace but grotesque, because he had acted from no other motive than the love of evil.

A spacious lawn fronted my childhood home, and in the middle of it grew a large pear tree. I was raised in Snowflake, a Mormon village in northeastern Arizona. My home was a two-story structure built in pioneer times of native red brick. A silo, corrals, and barn were at the back, and an ample vegetable garden to the side. One summer morning when I was small I stood at the crack of a door peering at my mother, who sat in a rocking chair breastfeeding my infant sister. Mother covered her breast with her apron and called me into the room. I entered, crestfallen and redfaced.

"Won't you be a clean boy?" Mother asked. "You mustn't peek at Mama. God doesn't like dirty boys." She sighed. "I've told you a dozen times, and now I'm going to punish you. You go outside and wait. Don't you come back into the house until I call you."

I sat on the stone steps and cried. Father came along and, because of my contrition, took me to Uncle Omar's farm. I sat by him in the pickup and the world seemed fine. Father went off with Uncle Omar while Cousin Rebecca took me into her charge. She had tight braids and plump brown cheeks. She showed me some baby cats in a currant patch and then took me into the barn loft. We came to a high, hidden corner. Rebecca sat in the hay with crossed legs, and I could see her panties.

"Do you have a tinky?" she asked.

"I don't know," I said. "What's a tinky?"

"Well, you've got one. I've got something, too. Do you want to see it?"

When I understood her proposal, I was feverish with excitement and pleasure. A day or two later I made the same proposal to the anemic little girl from across the street whose name I do not remember. We went into the corn patch, but the corn wasn't high enough. Mother whipped me severely and sent me to my room for the remainder of the day. The next morning Mother was very cheerful and paid a great deal of attention to me. At midmorning she sat with me in the living room and read me a story from *The Children's Friend*. Then she pulled me halfway into her lap, pressed my head against her breast, and said, "Be Mama's sweet little boy." I nodded and everything seemed fine again.

It was late in the afternoon before I had time to myself. I wandered out onto the lawn and saw the pear tree, thick with leaves and half-grown pears. I climbed and climbed, higher than ever before, until I clung to frail branches in the top. Beyond the borders of the town I could see rolling plains silver with grass and purple with junipers and flecked and studded by knolls and mesas and buttes. To the north the land reached away to an imperceptible union with the sky. To the south it ended in a blue rim of mountains. I knew that thick stands of pine covered the mountains and in the deep, cool canyons aspen and fir trees grew. In some places there were lakes, and streams rushing with white water.

I had soared free like a bird. At a point in my climb I had passed beyond the realm where God and my mother were sovereign. I had heard that God would come on the morning of the Millennium in a blaze of withering glory to consume the wicked, but as I looked beyond the town the wild, open land seemed stable and friendly and self-existent. It seemed safe now to begrudge the thousand impositions of God and my mother. I had to kneel through two long family prayers each day, and under Mother's watchful eye I had to say my silent prayer both morning and night. I could not speak angry or obscene words. I had to take naps and wash dishes and stand behind the picket fence and watch Father drive away. I had to go to Primary, Sunday School, and Sacrament Meeting and sit through long lessons and interminable sermons. I could not spit or get into mud or play with cow manure. It seemed that any pleasure or delight I had was suspect and liable to prohibition. In the security of the pear tree I took revenge: I diverted myself with a fantasy about Rebecca. I was a scop and a minstrel, a poet without pen and paper; I created a narrative in which I performed heroic deeds and Rebecca lavished admiration and tenderness upon me and allowed me to see and fondle her body. Later, having come down from the tree, I seemed to those around me to be an obedient and Christian child, but in my wild heart I knew otherwise.

God tolerated Augustine's willfulness for forty years, but mine he pruned away when I had no more than become a man.

When I was eighteen and out of high school, my father's friend Will Hamilton offered me a job at a dollar ten an hour, setting chokers in his logging operation. Will had built a sawmill near Highway 60 on the Apache Indian reservation; on the high ridges ten miles southeastward, he had a logging contract on fifty thousand acres of green and burned pine. My job was for the summer, and I was to save money to help myself enter Brigham Young University in the fall. With Father's signature, I bought on credit a deteriorating International pickup. I would keep bachelor's quarters in a tiny one-room cabin, and on Saturday nights I would drive home to spend the Sabbath with my parents and brothers and sisters.

On a hot Sunday afternoon Mother joined Father and me at the gate before our home. "I believe you forgot towels, Fremont," she said. "Here's a bundle of them. Please don't go dirty even if you are in the mountains. I don't suppose there will be any place where you can bathe. At least you can warm up a little water on your stove and take a spit bath from your basin. There's a freshly ironed shirt and a change of underwear for each day. Now for heaven's sake, change them when you're supposed to."

"Don't worry; I'll change," I said.

"I still think you should have got him a job here in town," Mother said.

"Jobs aren't that easy to get," Father said. "Outdoor jobs are good for a young fellow. He'll find out a lot about how the world runs."

"Yes, maybe he'll learn too much about how the world runs," Mother said. "I'm not sure it's the best environment for a Latter-day Saint boy."

"He won't have time for getting into trouble. Fresh air and work and plenty of good food—he'll sleep like a log, and he'll look back on this summer as one of the best times of his life."

"Well, I happen to know some things about Gentile standards in those mountain towns."

"There isn't a better Mormon in the world than Will Hamilton," Father said, "and I don't think his crew is so bad."

Mother came close to me and stroked my temple lightly. "Where has my little boy gone?"

"Don't make a funeral out of it, Mom," I said. "I'll be back on Saturday night."

"I can't see why you have to leave on Sunday," she said. "You could get up early and leave Monday morning. It isn't right to miss Sacrament Meeting.''

"I sure would like to get settled tonight," I said. "Work starts awfully early."

"You know what Latter-day Saint standards are," Mother said. "Don't forget them."

"I won't," I said, shaking my head emphatically.

"Please, Fremont," she went on, "say your prayers every night and morning. Think of God and He will think of you."

"I sure will," I said, and in a few minutes I was driving south toward Showlow and the mountains.

God holds the earth in vassalage. We call him Lord because we hold our lives and lands from Him. But if God chooses to neglect a demesne, it grows unruly and wild. There is in nature an impulse to be and to grow regardless of God. If you had asked for my conscious belief at eighteen, I would have said that God constantly superintends the tiniest pocket and farthest corner of the universe. But on that May evening when I drove into the blue mountains, my feelings were those of an outlaw coming into the security of an ungoverned land. It was my delight to be in a profane world.

It seemed no surprise to the men I worked with that I should be included among them, and I tried by my affability and hard work to keep their respect. At a quarter to seven each morning I put on my denim jacket and my straw hat, took my lunch pail, my gloves, and my canvas water bag, and walked to the mill. I rode to the woods in an old Navy ambulance driven by Roy Baker. Roy was the operator of one of Will's skid cats. Roy's tractor was equipped with a bulldozer and was sometimes used for roadbuilding. Ordinarily Roy and his tractor clanked and rumbled through the woods in search of logs to skid to the landings where the trucks were loaded. It was my duty to follow on foot and attach and release the cables by which the tractor dragged the logs. The days were hot, I worked with vigor, and when I returned to my cabin my entire body was black with sweat-caked dust. Each night I went into the canyon below the mill, stripped, and bathed in the cold, rushing water of the creek.

One day in June, Will asked me to drive my pickup to a logging operation near Vernon and bring back an acetylene welding outfit.

By early afternoon, after following three logging roads to their
ends, I found myself in Vernon and still ignorant of the whereabouts
of the welder. For lunch I had the choice of the grocery shelves in the
post office or a little cafe attached to the Texaco station on the highway. I went into the cafe. A girl, leaning behind the counter, closed
a book and looked at me. I searched my pockets and laid out
seventy-nine cents.

I said, "Young lady, you see here my total fortune. What can you
do for me?"

She was about my age, a little on the short side, and dressed in a
starched blouse, a denim skirt, and sandals. Her face was alert but
plain. I immediately ranked her among those girls useful for a
friendly talk but not pretty enough to be courted seriously.

She poked at the money with a finger and said, "I make out two
cheeseburgers and a glass of milk, which would be good for a growing boy."

"There not being anything but men at this counter, we will have a
7-Up. Proceed with the cheeseburgers."

Eyeing the jukebox, I said, "I'm impressed with this restaurant,
though it seems too bad there isn't any music."

She pushed two nickels apart from the coins I had placed on the
counter. I selected Hank Williams's "Lovesick Blues" and Moon
Mullican's "I'll Sail My Ship Alone," and in an instant the little
cafe was filled with guitar music and the laments of country singers.
The girl worked rhythmically at the grill. I saw that her legs were
tanned and very appealing. In a moment she placed the cheeseburgers before me.

"What's your name?" I asked.

"Annie Fergusson," she said. "And yourself?"

"Fremont H. Dunham. In the flesh."

"Want some coffee instead of that weak 7-Up?"

"I don't drink coffee."

"You a Mormon?"

"Yep."

"I'm a Baptist."

"Repent and be baptized, sister," I said, holding up a forefinger.

"Sure," she said, "you Mormons think all the rest of us are
pagans."

"I'm looking for Warren Jessup," I said. "He's got a welder I need. I've gone up every road in these mountains."

"You've got to go by our ranch," Annie said. "Warren's working east of Green's Peak."

"I didn't know your daddy was a rancher," I said.

"He leased this cafe to support the ranch, but all it does is keep me busy. It grossed ten dollars this morning. You sure you don't want some of this coffee?" She brought a pot over and poured a cup. I tasted it. "Gosh," I said, "that is nasty. Why do people drink it?"

"Dose it up with cream and sugar," she said and pushed them my way.

I tasted the coffee again. "That's tolerable, real tolerable."

"How come Mormons don't drink coffee?" she asked.

"Joseph Smith got a revelation from God called the Word of Wisdom. We don't smoke, we don't drink liquor, we don't drink tea and coffee, and we're just generally virtuous."

"Sure," she said. "However, I don't think you ought to drink that coffee if it hurts your conscience."

I pushed her hand away. "It's my first cup," I said. "I have fallen into evil company. Did you say your name is Delilah?" She laughed. "Here I am," I went on, "with my long flowing locks and my head in your lap, and you are about to cut off my hair and turn me over to the Philistines."

"I wouldn't do that to the man I loved."

"Say, those were mighty good cheeseburgers."

"You look like you need more. Are you sure you're not hungry?"

"Well, now that you mention it," I said, "I believe I could eat a bit more. I generally eat the wrappers off my candy bars."

She cut a big piece of pie, put on two scoops of ice cream, and poured a glass of milk. "A growing boy needs food," she said.

"Wait a minute," I said. "I couldn't be beholden to a Baptist."

"I insist. The management says it's okay to feed pie à la mode to the poor." I ate the pie heartily, and as I finished, she brought another scoop of ice cream. "I like to see calves and puppies grow," she added.

"I can tell you do," I said, "and I'm going to recommend this place to my friends." I got up and put on my hat. "Thank you kindly for this good food."

"How would you like it if I came along?" she asked. "I've got Daddy's Jeep. I don't get to drive it very often. Let's just roar up there and find old Jessup and we'll be back before you know it."

"I didn't think a little thing like you could drive a Jeep."

"I can wrassle anything that's got four legs or a steering wheel," she said. "I was born on a cattle drive."

"That could be," I said, "though from your delicate manners I took it you were born somewhere like Massachusetts."

"Don't be dumb," she said. "Come on; let's go. Here, take this." She handed me an encased rifle. "This is Daddy's deer gun. We'll knock off some jackrabbits while we drive."

In a moment we were speeding up the road, leaving behind a cloud of dust. Annie's hair whipped in the wind, her eyes glistened, and a smile played on her face. We drove through hills covered by tall grass and spotted with clumps of juniper and groups of grazing Herefords. Within half an hour we were among the pines in the high mountains. We found Jessup and loaded the welder into the back of the Jeep. Later, among the junipers again, Annie swung the Jeep off the road and dodged among the trees in pursuit of a jackrabbit. When the rabbit stopped, she took the rifle from its case, lifted it to her shoulder and fired. The rabbit burst apart.

"Gosh," I said. "Pretty good, except it was sitting. Drive on and give me that gun."

"Daddy'd beat the tar out of me if he knew I was knocking this grass down," she said. In a few minutes we picked up another jack. I put the gun to my shoulder, caught the running form in the scope, led a little, and pulled the trigger. The rabbit disintegrated in a shower of fur and bones.

"There," I said, "that's how it's done."

"You couldn't do that again," she said.

"Neither could you," I said. We looked at each other and burst out laughing.

When the welder was in my pickup, I swept off my hat, made a bow, and said, "Annie, it has been an honor."

"When you want a good cheeseburger, you come back," she said. She stepped closer. "I don't think your shirt has been ironed."

"I don't exactly live where you can iron things."

"Doesn't your mother iron them?"

"Well," I said, "Mother irons my shirts in turn. If I don't happen to want to wear the ones she's ironed, I have to take them unironed." I got into the pickup and started the engine. "Good-by," I said.

She stepped close to the window and said, "I would iron your shirts if you wanted me to."

Joseph Smith said that, in the beginning, there was inchoate matter and there were intelligences. One of these intelligences was superior, and He became God. He organized matter and made stars, suns, and worlds. He gave spiritual bodies to other intelligences, and they became His children in the pre-existence. Then, to give them a perfect being like His own, He prepared a mortal existence for them to test who would obey Him and who would not.

It is inchoate matter that troubles me. It is coeval with God. It does not owe its being to Him. It has an obduracy, an impulse of its own, a will to be other than what God wills. How do I otherwise account for myself at eighteen? I desired a world where omnipotence and immortality and love were mine without the subjugation of my will to any other, a world where happiness was free for the picking, like berries on a hillside.

A prayer and a machine derive from the same human motives. A machine can be a kind of pagan prayer, a worshipful call for the power to change reality. I was entranced by the machines I found in the mountains, and Will Hamilton made it easy for me to master them. Sometimes he pulled his pickup into the landing where Roy and I ate lunch and, with a happy greeting, joined us. While he ate his sandwiches and drank his fruit juice, he explained the planetary gears in the steering mechanism of an International tractor or the Eaton axle of a logging truck. He encouraged me to experiment with any idle machine, and, while Roy looked on with a frown, Will showed me how to operate the skid cat and its bulldozer.

My feelings for machines were intimate, personal, mystical. Awe came over me when I sat on the tread of the tractor and contemplated its idling diesel. A warm wind from the radiator fan brushed my face, and the purr of the engine filled my ears. I knew that the static, imperturbable exterior of the engine was an illusion: hidden within its cast-iron casing, water gushed and honey-golden fuel sprayed into the cylinder heads and exploded, driving the pistons down upon the crankshaft with volcanic heat and clamor and power. It was also an act of communion when I watched the great circular mill saw. Balanced on its arbor, it was as high as a man. A hundred filed, offset teeth gleamed on its circumference. When the muffled diesel behind it worked and the broad rubber belt whirred on pulleys, the great blade sang with an almost imperceptible timbre, like crystal that has been lightly struck. In motion, the teeth blurred into the iridescence of hummingbird wings. At the elevation of the sawyer's finger, the carriage man ratcheted a log into position, and suddenly it hurtled into the saw. The teeth shrieked, the sawdust spurted, and irresistibly a plank fell away.

In that early summer it seemed that I sat at a laden table and dished rich food onto my plate. Beside the machines there was wilderness. I did not think then about ecology or pollution or dwindling resources; the felled trees, the skid paths, the dugways and roads seemed only a minor and temporary irritation upon the face of the wilderness. Water, wind, and sky, the animals, the grass, the trees, each in its own kind and species existed proportionately and impressed its character upon me. How can I summarize wilderness? It is an entity composed of infinite variety. A single ant, a fern, a cluster of pine needles speaks, and an attentive person can listen endlessly. When I found a seep of water in a narrow, dark canyon, it was like the face of a friend I had not seen in years. My lust for sensation, for color and texture and configuration, was fed by the glint of dew on bending grass or by the stark red-rust branches of the manzanita. I respected all trees, but I venerated the ponderosa pines, as if they were wise and ancient parents upon whom I continued to depend. They were tall and straight, and when all engines were quiet and a wind blew, the pines swayed and an immense orchestration of soft sighing lifted over the mountains. Once, from a high, open ridge that overlooked all others, I watched a thunderstorm advance across the land. The moving column of cloud filled half the sky, boiling upward thirty thousand feet into billows of the purest white. At its base all was dark and misty. Lightning fractured the sky, and thunder rolled and reverberated through the mountains. I took my hat in my hands and let the wind whip my hair, and I watched a wall of rain come ever closer; when at last it reached me, I stood drenched and exultant. It was a pagan worship. I loved the earth, and, walking abroad on its wild face, I believed in my own immensity, omnipotence, and immortality.

On a Saturday night in late June I sat eating my supper at home. At the other end of the table Father prepared a Sunday School lesson with the aid of the Scriptures and a pad of paper. Mother ironed, and shirts and pants hung about the room.

"I can't believe how dirty you get," she said.

"It washes off."

"Off you," she said, "but not off your clothes. Even your underwear is black. Are you sure you change every day?"

I lifted my arm to the square. "On my honor."

Father said, "I'm sorry to say that I don't like this Scripture, and I wish it weren't in the lesson manual."

"I'm not sure it's our choice to like or dislike a Scripture," Mother said.

"Listen," Father went on. " 'But he that shall blaspheme against the Holy Ghost hath never forgiveness but is in danger of eternal damnation.' "

"That means the sons of perdition," Mother said. "There won't be many of them."

"I know," Father said, "but I thought Mormons didn't believe in damnation. There are three degrees of glory, and the unworthy inherit one of the lesser."

The iron sizzled; my knife and fork clattered. "Well," said Mother, "there really is something called damnation, whether you like it or not. If the Holy Ghost bears witness to you and then you fail, you are cast into outer darkness."

"How do you know if the Holy Ghost bears witness?" I asked.

"Oh, you'll know, don't worry about that," Mother said. "Amos, did you know that the black slugs are taking the asparagus again? Do you think we could find something to poison them with?"

"Don't sprinkle the plants. Just irrigate them."

"I haven't sprinkled them," Mother said. "Fremont, do you want some pie?"

"You bet," I said.

"Can't you say *certainly*?" Mother asked.

"Certainly," I said. "How about some ice cream on it? Have you got some?"

"It isn't a matter of whether I have some. It seems funny to put one dessert on top of another."

"It won't hurt him," Father said. "He's lost ten pounds."

"All right," Mother said.

"How about two or three scoops?" I said.

The next morning I awoke when Father stuck his head through my doorway and asked, "Do you want to go to Priesthood Meeting with me, Fremont?"

"Yeah, I'll come along," I mumbled.

I heard Father turn on the shower, and I stretched out in bed. I had a happy feeling, though for a moment I did not quite know why. Then I remembered that I had dreamed about Annie Fergusson. In the dream I saw myself in the woods. Seeing the flash of a running deer, I turned aside from the skid path and entered a thicket of jack pines. Without surprise, I saw Annie among the small trees. A beam of light, falling through the lacy boughs of a single old fir, sparkled on her brown hair; she wore high heels and hose and a suit that matched her hair. I looked down in shame at my sweat-stained shirt and my soiled Levi's. The scene changed, and I saw that I wore a suit and tie. Annie and I stood in the muted light of a high school gymnasium where a dance band played soft, mellow music. Her hand clasped mine, and as we faced one another, ready to dance, the dream ended. Instantly upon remembering it I was aware that I was in love with Annie—deeply and without reservation. I was overwhelmed. This cluttered bedroom where I had slept for so many years seemed too familiar and commonplace for such a momentous event. I had been taught, by the conversation of friends, by books and movies, by old couples who after fifty years still called each other sweetheart, that love would perfect my life, that the reciprocal exchange of affection and passion between me and a lovely woman would bring a total and lasting happiness. Irresistibly, I believed in

Annie. With her my life would drift in Eden, where hunger is fed and thirst is slaked, where desire leads inevitably to fulfillment, where no matter how colossal the aspiration, there is a joy equal to it.

I went to Priesthood Meeting, and I sat with Father and Mother through the opening exercises of Sunday School. I went to my class and sat through half the lesson. Then, without a word, I stood up and left. I went home, packed my clothes and my groceries, left a note for Father and Mother, and drove away. An hour and a half later I was on the porch of the Fergusson ranch house. A boy answered my knock.

"Does Annie Delilah Fergusson live here?" I asked.

"Well, Annie lives here," the boy said.

She came to the door. "I heard that, and it's really dumb. Come in. What are you doing so far away from home?"

"I wondered if you iron shirts on Sunday."

"Sure," she said. "Bring them in."

A heavy woman with grey hair and a kind smile stood within an inner doorway. "Mother," Annie said, "this is Fremont Dunham. He said he would eat supper with us and go to evening service. Didn't you, Fremont?"

"I don't want to put you out."

"You won't be any bother," Mrs. Fergusson said. "Please stay."

I fit into the family instantly. Mr. Fergusson kept me occupied for almost two hours in talk about Will Hamilton's logging operation and with a backyard inspection of a brood of white turkeys. After the church service he crowded his family and me into an old sedan and took us across his holdings to show me his Herefords. Later we sat in the living room and Mrs. Fergusson brought cookies and coffee. Annie poured a cup and handed it to me with a question on her face. I took it without a word.

I am surprised when I remember how little time I actually spent with Annie. For the five or six weeks after I first knew that I loved her, I tucked her in between everything else I was committed to. I was in the woods from dawn till dark six days a week, and I still spent Saturday nights and Sundays with my family. Will gave me a day off for the Fourth of July, and I took Annie to the rodeo in

Showlow. He gave me another day off for the Mormon Pioneer Day celebration. I did not tell my parents, and Annie and I rode on her father's horses among the foothills of the mountains. A thunderstorm came by in the afternoon. We huddled under a rocky ledge and watched the wind-whipped clouds race across the sky. The grass moved in broad undulations, and the earth seemed immense and absolutely free.

Once or twice a week I drove to see Annie in the late evening. Sometimes we were sensible and I stayed only an hour or two. We often drove along the back roads in my pickup and returned to her kitchen to have sandwiches and coffee. Sometimes we took a blanket and went to a little swale Annie knew. Cottonwood boughs hung intimately over a carpet of reeds and grass, and the frogs bellowed incessantly at night. We lay on the blanket and talked and looked at the brilliant sky. Later, when we parted on the porch of her house, we kissed each other a few times. I did not ask for more because I feared something cataclysmic.

In those weeks of midsummer I knew Annie best and most closely in my fantasies. During the long, vacant afternoons as I trudged behind the tractor, or when I lay in my bunk awaiting sleep, or while I sat in Sacrament Meeting trying to ignore the sermon, I thought of Annie. Again I was a scop and a minstrel. I drew a setting and created a plot peopled with characters, of whom Annie and I were the principals. The narratives were numerous, but in them all I was the master of great machines, and I loved Annie and she loved me, and she admitted me to the intimacy of her body. In justice to myself, I will say that my fantasies were not so far from what might have been. On any day or night, my fantasy might simply be that I was the owner of a fleet of logging trucks. The men who worked for me respected me, and the people in the county roundabout admired me. At evening I came out of the mountains driving a huge truck from whose upright stacks blue exhaust streamed. The hood of the truck was green and shiny, and on its radiator cap a chrome bulldog leaped forward. I parked the truck beside the house and stepped from the cab. I wore an aluminum safety hat cocked at a self-confident angle. I had a flannel shirt with sleeves rolled up, and on my feet I wore high-heeled logging boots. Two little children ran from the house, and I picked them up and hugged them. Annie came out, I kissed her, and we all went in to supper. There was no end to that happiness. There was neither sickness nor grief nor infidelity nor guilt nor boredom nor depression. The skies were spacious and blue; sunshine was everywhere. It was summer forever in the mountains of Arizona.

I do not think people pray because they ought to pray. They pray because there is something they need. "Say your prayers, Fremont," my mother had said, and of course I did not. The woods were wild and bright, and the men and machines seemed stable and self-existent. That is how I thought of Roy Baker. He was dour and habitual. He discussed our work only in brief explanatory terms. He listened to country-western music while we drove to and from the woods, and he seemed to have no interest in the weather or in his wife and children or in movies, sports, or scandals. I did not like him, but neither did I resent him, since he found my work acceptable. He seemed fixed and permanent, like a knoll on the landscape of my childhood.

One hot afternoon in August, Roy accidentally allowed the bulldozer to brush against a dead, weathered tree. There was nothing I could do to help. The snag shuddered; its top leaned askew and fell. Roy cut the throttle and tried to jump. I raced to the tractor and leaped upon the track. Roy was pinned beneath the shattered tree top. The ribs on his left side were popped and twisted like wire; his lung protruded; blood dribbled from his nose. He was dead. A Scripture filed through my mind, as if someone were reading in a calm, clear voice: "Rather fear him which is able to destroy both soul and body in hell. Are not the sparrows sold for a farthing? And not one of them shall fall on the ground without your Father's notice." I had an illumination. I perceived that the mountains were not wild and vacant; I knew God was everywhere. I jumped to the ground and stood paralyzed by surging terror. I would have run if I had known where to go.

In a moment my manliness returned. I levered the snag off Roy and dragged him into the shade of a juniper. I covered the blood on the seat and floorboard of the tractor with pine needles. The tractor idled peacefully, but the bulldozer still rested against the snag, and the slightest vibration could bring down another portion of the rotted tree. The trick lay with the fulcrum of the tractor. Watching the snag intently, I put the tractor into a reverse gear, immobilized the track next to the tree, and allowed the other track to move slightly. The bulldozer swung the merest inch away from the tree, but that was enough. Beyond the snag, I lowered the bulldozer and cleared a rough road to the landing.

I was a pallbearer at Roy's funeral. Father and Mother went with me to the community church in Pinetop and later took me back to Snowflake. I drove around town in the late afternoon looking for friends, but I found none. After supper I sat on the porch swing. In a while Father and Mother came out. It was a cool, pleasant evening.

Mother asked, "How's Annie?"

"OK, so far as I know."

"You don't talk about her much."

"There's not too much to say about her."

"Does she ever think about joining the church?"

I shrugged my shoulders.

"Have you asked her?"

"Well, not exactly."

Water gurgled in the irrigation ditch, and crickets chirped. Then I realized that Mother was crying. "I just don't know what I would do," she said, "if one of my children should marry outside the Covenant."

"Good grief, Mom," I said, "who's talking about marrying anyone? Annie is just a good friend."

"That's deceitful, Fremont," Mother said with passion. "You don't drive sixty miles four times a week just to be with a good friend. We haven't said anything, but what on earth do you expect? You can't see a girl that often at your age without it leading to something."

"I don't see her four times a week," I said. I got up and paced across the porch. I was like a bear at bay, beleaguered and confused.

"I've got to go," I said. "I've got to get back to the mill." I went to my room for my hat and jacket. Coming down the stairs, I heard Father and Mother in the kitchen. Mother was sobbing.

My sister Julia stood by my pickup. "Well," she said, "aren't you proud of yourself?"

"Is that all you've got to say?"

"I don't admire your thinking ability one little bit," Julia said. "Do you really want to trade eternity for a Gentile girl with tight pants and a big bust?"

"You shut your mouth," I said. "Someday somebody's going to put a washtub in it."

Father came from the house and told Julia to go in. "I'm sorry, Fremont," he said. "I don't think we quite knew how far things had gone. How about it? Will you bring her home to see us? We'll be on good behavior and leave religion out of it. If you love Annie, we want to love her, too."

Will raised me twenty-five cents an hour and put me on the tractor in Roy's place. With a little help from Will on the construction of switchbacks, I built a road into a steep canyon and along its bottom as far as Will's contract went. The canyon was a two-year-old burn. It was an eerie, barren place. There were whole hillsides of charred, skeletal jack pines and baked, denuded manzanita. I worked under an unusual and inexplicable tension. Setting chokers for myself, I stacked the logs in the landings at almost the rate at which Roy and I had brought them in together. My very fatigue kept me from sleeping well at night. I was in a growing mood for something decisive, and I had an intense need for Annie.

I drove to Vernon on a Friday night and found her at a wedding in the Baptist church. She was very dressed up and pretty. Afterward we took a blanket and went to the little swale. After the heat of the scorched canyon, the night air was delicious to my bare arms. I lay and Annie sat, and I listened to her talk for a while.

At last I said, "Do you smell the rain?"

She sniffed and said no.

"It's somewhere over the mountains," I said. "I can smell the rain and the pines."

"I smell them."

"They remind me of you," I said.

She laughed. "Do I smell like pine gum and turpentine?"

"Not turpentine," I said. "You smell good. Do you know something? You are better than I am."

"That isn't true."

"People respect you. I saw it at the church tonight."

"They can't find anyone else to play the piano."

I sat up on the blanket and said, "After lunch yesterday, I took a nap. When I woke up, I rolled on my side and there, right in my face, was a clump of Indian paintbrush. It had about fifty scarlet and red and orange blossoms. It made me think about Moses and the burning bush. That bush Moses saw must have been like a juniper burning at night when kids on a picnic set a tree on fire; maybe it was white hot like an acetylene torch. And Moses took off his shoes because it was a holy place. When I woke up and saw that Indian paintbrush, I thought: I could take off my shoes, too; there is somebody I would do it for."

Annie was silent. "I'm trying to say something to you," I said. "I don't know how to say it." It was as if a boulder were buried within me and I had no shovel to dig it out.

Annie put her hand on my arm. I said, "I told my parents that you were my friend. They knew it was more than that."

She leaned against me and we lay down. She pressed her face into my neck. Her hair tumbled across my face.

"I love you," I said. Blood roared in my ears and my stomach throbbed.

"No one else has ever said that to me," she whispered.

We lay for a long time. Wind stirred the cottonwoods and distant thunder rumbled. Without a word or any notable gesture from Annie, I knew I had permission to do the cataclysmic thing I had feared. My innocence lay entirely within my own hands. There was no barrier, no gate or door, nothing solid and immovable to protect me. It was as easy as breathing to unbutton her blouse and unzip her skirt. It was nothing at all to slide my hand along her thighs. With the softest and kindest murmur, Annie unfastened her bra and slipped off her panties.

Mormons cannot ordinarily admit that moral volition is an illusion. They prefer to think that the choice between good and evil is as voluntary and accessible as turning on a radio. I do not say so to my fellow Mormons, but I am attracted to Augustine's idea that he was bound to his perversity until God had touched him. In his carnal youth he could not break from his evil will, and even his prayers went in this manner: "Grant me chastity and continence, O God, but not yet."

After leaving Annie, I grieved for my innocence. When I slept my mind swirled with dreams. A faceless woman leaned over me. Her nipple was cratered, as if it had been countersunk with a pipe reamer. I saw brown water flowing between rows of half-grown corn, and my feet bogged helplessly in the mud. I fell into a ditch; I clung to a headgate; a man slammed the gate shut on my fingers; a current of dark water whirled me into a siphon.

It was little better to be awake. Throughout the day, images of self-mutilation occurred to me. I saw my tendons skewered and my eviscerated body, with bare and bloody ribs, hung out like a butchered hog. I saw myself before an acetylene torch; I had placed my fingers into its bright flame until they broiled and bubbled into stubs.

As a new week came and I performed my work, I sought ways to do penance. I assumed an attitude of self-execration. I abused myself for my faults and asserted my incompetence. I prepared plain and tasteless food; I worked without rest and went without water as long as possible. I breathed dust and diesel fumes with a vigorous will, and I welcomed the hottest and most interminable part of each day. At last it seemed to me that I had bought back my innocence. My good cheer began to return, and I felt stronger and more confident. I was sure I could bury my single failure in the past.

It was again a Friday evening when I drove to Vernon. I wanted to see Annie very much. I wanted to prove how well things would go for us and how simply and purely we could conduct ourselves. We went to St. Johns to a dance. A western band played raucous music, and young couples, clad in Levi's and bright full skirts, hooted and stamped and shuffled their way around the hall. It was fun, and afterward Annie and I had a hamburger in an all-night cafe.

Annie's eyes sparkled as she told me a story. "I said, Jerry, damn you, get out of this corral and quit stirring up the cows or I'm going to bust you one good. He just stood there and laughed his toothless little laugh, so I stripped down hard on the udder and filled up a teat till it bulged and then I let him have it. I squirted him right in the nose and he went bawling into the house. When I finished milking, Mom tried to act mad, but she wasn't.''

We laughed. It seemed a long time since I had felt so relaxed and happy. As we drove to the ranch Annie sat close to me, and I knew that I loved her very much. We stood on the porch and I kissed her. I told her twenty times that I was leaving, but I couldn't go. At last I unbuttoned her blouse and slid my hand into her bra. She removed my hand and led me from the porch. We took a blanket from the seat of the family car and crossed the road into the junipers. For many weeks I existed in this manner, my life a harrowing cycle of penance and fornication.

At first, September was a beautiful month. The skies were bright and the aspens turned gold. In the mornings, frost sparkled on the grass and mist hung on the sides of the high canyons. But at the equinox a week-long storm moved in. On the day the rain began, I put on my denim jacket and continued my work. Cold rivulets ran down my back and water sloshed in my shoes. Near eleven o'clock, Will came by in his pickup.

He crawled onto the tractor with me and said, "Boy, why don't you get out of the rain?"

"Got work to do," I said.

"This storm isn't going to quit for a while," he said. "We'd better get out of the woods while we can. Why don't you take the dozer and help the trucks up the canyon? Then you and the limbers better get in the old ambulance and come on out."

Clouds hovered close, and the wind whipped rain into our faces. "Let me say something to you," Will said. "It really ain't any of my business. This lady from Vernon came by my house Sunday—Mrs. Fergusson. I know you've been going with Annie, and I heard the boys josh you about her, but I told Mrs. Fergusson I didn't know anything about it. I guess she and her husband are pretty concerned."

I fidgeted with the throttle and said nothing. "When you came on last summer," Will continued, "you talked some of quitting in the fall and going to BYU."

"Dad and Mom aren't very happy about that," I said, "but I

don't feel settled enough to be going off to college."

"Well, that's OK," Will said. "You've got a job with me until the woods close for the winter. In fact, if you want to kind of throw in with me permanent, I'll keep you on at the mill."

I nodded my thanks. Will patted my arm. "You know," he said, "you're a Mormon and I'm a Mormon, but there are worse things than marrying outside your religion. The time comes when you're going with a girl that you ought to get married. If it's a case of money, don't worry. I don't feel good about what I'm paying you. You've proved yourself and I'll raise you." He squeezed my arm and jumped off the tractor. Like my father, Will Hamilton was one of the good men of the earth, and I try to remember him when I hire a man at my yard.

I felt elevated for the first time in weeks. I had come to a decision. I would marry Annie. I set my doubt and guilt at defiance, and I worked through the day in the cold rain with a fierce exultation. I pushed the trucks up not just one but many hills, and I did not get into my cabin until after dark. Annie expected me, and I left the cabin and drove to Showlow. The neon lights of its motels and cafes glittered on the mirror of the wet pavement. I pulled into a Shell station and filled my tank with gasoline.

The man at the cash register said, "That will be four dollars and fifteen cents."

As I reached for my wallet, I idly contemplated the act of getting into my pickup and driving on to Vernon. Suddenly I felt an immense resistance to that act. I was puzzled. It was as if I had a forgotten obligation, a duty that required me to go elsewhere. I scanned my mind to see whether I had promised my parents that I would return home this evening, or whether I had told Will that I would pick up a spare part in McNary. I could think of nothing.

"Can I help you with something else?" the man asked.

Without warning or premonition, I knew that I did not love Annie. A finger had pressed a switch; a light had gone out. Annie suddenly seemed plain and featureless, uninteresting like sand in the bed of a wash, or undelectable like last year's apple left in the basket. I did not want to see her, to touch her, to laugh with her. I had put her away.

"Is there something else I can help you with?"

As I struggled to refine my responses, to grasp as precisely as possible the nature of this strange and unexpected catastrophe, I knew that, if I did not love Annie, at least I wanted to love her. Hard upon repulsion came grief. I felt as if it were Annie, not Roy, whom I had seen buried. I felt as if I had looked into a coffin and had seen her white and attenuated face, as if I had watched people gently lower the lid and tighten down chrome-headed screws, as if I now contemplated the implacable silence of a heaped-up barrow of earth. I became angry. By what stretch of the law, by what misinterpretation of human rights was I bereft of a joy so immeasurable? Who was it who trifled with my dignity and aspiration?

"That will be four dollars and fifteen cents," the man said.

I looked around in surprise, as if I had just awakened from sleep. "Sure," I said. I handed the man four dollars from my wallet and found change in my pocket.

I did not go to Vernon. I turned south and drove for many hours along the back roads of the mountains. It was a solitary and eerie journey. The logging hamlets and the Indian towns were dark and silent. The road was a glimmering burrow through crowding ranks of trees. Rain beat on the cab of my pickup; the single wiper whined incessantly. My mind raced. Everything certain, calculable, and fixed had toppled like brick walls in an earthquake. I could draw only one conclusion: I could not play chess against God. He never gamed, and even if He did, He made and broke rules as He pleased. By fair means or foul, He would snatch away my pawn, my bishop, my queen. God ruled not only the world beyond me, but the world within me as well. Matter could exercise its willful and inchoate impulse only as God allowed. There was no stronghold where outlaws could gather in security; there was no profane land, no godless paradise. Wilderness was an illusion, and the love of a man for a woman was nothing more than a peanut shell that God shredded between His fingers. God had cornered me at last. If I hoped to love Annie, I would have to enter His market. I would have to make my bids and present my offers and see what bargains God might be willing to make.

Near four in the morning, I came onto Highway 60 fifteen miles south of the mill. I suppose that, in a sense, I had been praying all night, but it occurred to me now that I must humble myself and kneel. I parked the pickup along the highway and walked through the rain into the dark trees. I knelt in the mud and for the first time in my life I prayed with fervor. The answer was no.

When I came to my cabin, I realized that for the last hundred yards the lights of an automobile had followed me. It was Annie. "I didn't know where your cabin was," she said, "so I waited until you came through the cattleguard."

We went into the cabin and I lit the lantern. "I worried about you when you didn't come," Annie said.

"Yes," I said, "I think I am sick." I sat on the bunk. Annie sat beside me and looked at me with anxious, searching eyes.

"Maybe I ought to fix us something to eat," I said.

"Let me do it," she said. "You are so wet and cold. I'll get you something warm." She reached out her hand and gently pulled my face against hers. She spoke in scarcely more than a whisper. "Love sanctifies. Don't you believe that?"

"I don't know," I murmured.

"I don't think we are vile and abhorrent," she went on. "We are lifted up by how we feel for each other. I have prayed for God to signify if it is wrong for me to be happy, but I am still happy, very happy. I am quite sure now that I will have a baby."

We sat silent for a long time, pressed tightly together. Then Annie said, "You are crying."

I nodded and said, "I don't love you."

Her body became tense, and she seemed very small and fragile. "Please, Fremont," she said. The rain drummed on the cabin roof. The lantern sputtered; a moth whirred and butted about the bright globe. "What shall I do?" she asked.

"I don't know," I said. "It's as if you are dead."

"I'll be a Mormon if you want me to."

I shook my head. "I just don't love you."

She pulled away. Tear tracks gleamed on her cheeks. "Won't you try?" she asked.

"Yes," I said, "I will try."

Annie and I were married, and we lived together almost three months in a small house in Showlow. The best thing to be said for our listless marriage is that we were kind to each other. In December Father drove Annie to the Fergusson ranch, and I have never seen her since. For a couple of years Father paid support for Annie and our son. Then Annie married a man from Albuquerque and had another child. That marriage ended in divorce, but, soon after, Annie married her present husband, a cotton farmer from Yuma, Arizona. She has had four more children.

I left Arizona in January and enrolled for the winter quarter at Brigham Young University. I went into the Army, returned to the university, and completed a business degree. During my last year at Brigham Young I married LaDene. She comes from a good Latter-day Saint family in Eugene, Oregon. We have five children. LaDene and I are close, and we are very involved with our children. After my graduation we moved to Salt Lake City, where I worked for a while for the A & B Building Supply. About thirteen years ago I started a small enterprise of my own. It has grown, and both the yard and the hardware store will be free of debt within a few years.

I see evidence that people respect me as an honest and righteous man. That reputation has come because I try to serve God in all aspects of my life. I work hard and I try to be fair in my business dealings. LaDene and I have family prayer in our home, and I say my silent prayers. I pay a tenth of my income as a tithing to the church; I pay 6 or 7 percent more for welfare, ward maintenance, and building projects. I keep the Word of Wisdom, and I attend Priesthood Meeting, Sunday School, Sacrament Meeting, and any other meetings to which my special duties may require me to go. I try to suppress anger, I use no obscene language, and I engage in no conversation that might injure the reputation of another person. I have twice been a counselor in the bishopric of my ward, and I am presently a high councilman in my stake. I am, I hope, a credit to my parents. I am happy that they lived long enough to be proud of me.

I must come now to Augustine, whose book, accidentally put into my hands, has stirred my memories. He and I are brothers. Like him, I was converted at the price of pain.

The conversion of Augustine was so profound and complete that he narrowed his passion and love to God alone. I read: "But I do long for thee, O Righteousness and Innocence, so beautiful and comely to all virtuous eyes—I long for thee with an insatiable satiety.'' Every page, every paragraph, almost every sentence that he wrote reflects his single-minded devotion. By every conceivable figure and metaphor, by the heaped-up adjectives of praise, by every comparison and superlative that he could devise, he sang the greatness and goodness of God.

I have asked myself whether Augustine was correct in this. The restored Gospel teaches that God is not so jealous. I do not think God resents the feelings I have for the tools in my hardware store, for the ledgers that show I am prospering, for my automobile and my house, for my wife and children and friends. I may love, with strong and full heart, whatever God allows me to love. But if I love otherwise, then even love is corrupt.

The love of God is obedience. Like Augustine, I know that God will not be scorned. If it suits Him, He will feed me tragedy on the instant. He will shatter me, like a boy dropping an icicle on a pavement; He will break me, like a housewife who holds a green bean in her fingers and with no effort snaps it in two. There will be Judgment, and when it comes, I will be put into the fiery furnace and whatever is base and impure in me will be burned away and I will be the pure metal that God desires me to be.

I will speak honestly.

Augustine's mother wanted him to marry, if at all, only to his advantage. He in fact never married, for when at middle age he became engaged to a proper woman, God struck him, and Augustine gave himself to the priesthood and a life of celibacy. But in his carnal youth he kept a mistress. She must have been a woman of warmth and intelligence, because Augustine lived with her for many years and had a son by her. When at last he thought of marriage he sent her away, keeping their son with him. Considering his conversion, why should it matter that he sent away a woman of such lowly status that she was not worthy of marriage? Yet I cannot remove her from my mind. I see that, beyond his lust, Augustine loved her. I read again: ''My mistress, being torn from my side as a hindrance to my marriage, my heart which clave unto her was torn and wounded and bleeding. And she returned to Africa, vowing unto Thee, O God, never to know any other man." What thoughts came to those three, to Augustine, the one he loved, their son? How could Augustine swallow his anger?

Sometimes, when I am awakened in the night by the wail of a locomotive or the barking of a dog and my Christian will is at its lowest, I think of Annie. I remember her clearly. I see her brown knees beneath the hem of her denim skirt. I remember her happy laughter and the glint of the sun upon her hair while we loped horses across the grass and through the junipers. Though I am ashamed to say it, I remember in the cup of my hand the weight of her soft, round breast. God will exact payment from me for these memories; after the purging of Judgment, I will have them no longer. It is part of my perversity that this very thought makes them more precious.

From time to time over the years I entertained a fantasy in which my son came to see me. He is twenty-three now and has never come, and I have laid that fantasy aside. There is another fantasy that still visits me in the deep night while I await the return of sleep. Annie and I are walking toward each other on a high, open ridge on Will Hamilton's old logging contract. It does not matter how we have come there or where we will go. In the canyons below us are thick stands of ponderosa. To the south, ridges and buttes recede into blue infinity. Across the expanse a storm moves, and the mountains rumble with distant thunder and the wind is fresh with the scent of rain. Annie and I walk closer; at last we are face to face. Like me, she is older and heavier, but something about her warms me. I say, "Hello, Annie," and she says, "Hello, Fremont."

I say, "I ask your forgiveness. You deserved better than I gave. I did not know that God would hang me on a trellis of His own choosing and prune away that part of me that loves you. But until that pruning is complete, it comforts me to know that, somewhere on the face of this broad earth, you are still alive."

Annie says, "We had better go," and I say, "Yes." But I see by her face that she has been touched.

Trinity

On a winter afternoon Jamie Bolander wandered cheerlessly through the halls of the Louvre. The silent, impassive guards and the occasional clusters of subdued tourists did nothing to raise his spirits. Jamie had heard that art offered a kind of salvation. By moments, standing before a famous masterpiece like the *Nike of Samothrace* or the *Mona Lisa*, he was stirred by respect and awe. But for the most part the paintings and statues by which he strolled were potent with threats and accusations. His mind seethed with images from canvas and stone. Beyond counting, Madonnas and Apollos, saints and nudes, dukes and peasants, popes and satyrs stepped forth to condemn Jamie Bolander.

Jamie had been haunted throughout much of his life by an inexpressible anxiety which he assumed arose from a disjunction between him and God. At eighteen he had joined the Mormons and had gone to Utah, to the dismay of his Presbyterian parents, who remained in Pennsylvania. At twenty-one he accepted a mission call, thinking that he could find assurance in the consecrated life of a missionary. After a year in the mission his anxiety intensified. Late one night in Brussels, about three months before he came to Paris, Jamie was riding with his companion on a tram near the Palais de Justice. He was very tired from having walked the streets all day, knocking on doors and taking his turn at delivering a memorized message. Across the aisle was a handsome blond young man who swayed with the lurch of the tram. Languorously Jamie allowed his eyes to return time and again to the face of the youth, whose cheeks were round and full and whose brows made a striking arch over his clear blue eyes. All at once Jamie felt a surge of horror. Without warning, he had understood the mystery of his life: he desired men.

Depressed by the Louvre, Jamie wondered where else he might go to spend the afternoon. He could not bear the idea of returning to the mission home so early. Les Invalides, the Sacré-Coeur, the Sainte-Chapelle—he thought of these and a dozen other places, none of which promised comfort on this misting winter day. Jamie turned a corner into another hall of the Louvre. In the center of the hall, sitting alone on a padded bench, was a missionary whom he had met upon his arrival from Belgium the previous evening. The woman, Laura Greenhalgh, had been recently transferred to the mission home from the French Midi. She wore the same long grey coat, buttoned to her chin, which by some whim she had worn in the warm rooms of the mission home. There was an ominous eccentricity about her. Jamie stared a moment across the hall at the profile of her emaciated face. Her skin seemed more sallow and her cheek more hollow than he remembered from having seen her at breakfast that morning. The missionaries on the staff of the mission home told a curious story about her. She had been called in from the field for observation; very likely she would be returned prematurely to Utah. Her former companion had suffered a nervous collapse which she attributed to Laura's refusal to keep mission rules. Laura had come under the influence of an Austrian residing in Marseille. At first he seemed interested in the Gospel, but then it became apparent that he had a religious cult of his own. Laura had committed the immense indiscretion of attending meetings of his cult without her companion. There was a possibility that Laura had violated the law of chastity. In any event, she was at the mission home in a condition of discipline.

Laura glanced toward Jamie but did not seem to recognize him. The front view of her long, gaunt face touched Jamie with an incomprehensible sympathy. He approached her, stood silently a moment, then said, "Do you remember me? I'm the missionary who is being transferred to Lausanne. I have been to the Swiss embassy today, applying for a visa."

Laura put her hands into her coat pockets and pressed her arms against her body. She glanced at Jamie without surprise and spoke as if the two of them were in the middle of a conversation. "The problem with the French is filth. Did you ever see such a dirty country? Grimy streets, stairwells stinking of urine, cockroaches in every kitchen. I wouldn't live in most French cities for any amount of money. And if you want to see the worst, go to Perpignan."

"I could recommend some cities in Belgium for dirt," Jamie said. "Try Charleroi."

"The French are obscene; really, they are enamoured of whoredoms," Laura went on. "Their saving grace is Camembert cheese. And I love their bread, though I have bloody gums from chewing so many crusts." Then, abruptly: "Did you say Lausanne?"

He nodded. She said, "I was in Geneva first. You'll like the cheese in Switzerland. And the housewives cleaning their doorsteps. It's the German influence. Say what you want about the Germans, they're clean."

She shifted gingerly on the seat, carefully crossed her legs, and picked a bit of lint from her coat. "What do they expect to get from all this tracting the missionaries do? You go along, week in, week out, knocking on doors and saying"—she mimicked herself in a falsetto voice—"'We have an important message about God, which will save you; may we come in and tell it to you?' And the people look at you cold—they seem offended and insulted—and then they shut the door."

"A few people listen," Jamie said. "They are the ones who make it worthwhile."

"There are flamingos on the Mediterranean," Laura said. "Everyone raves about the sun in the Midi. But the flamingos are the exciting thing. I wouldn't ever have imagined them before. You can see them in the marshes by the sea. They are wild, like the seagulls on the lakes in Utah."

Impelled by her fervent, glistening eyes, Jamie imagined flamingos—stately, stilt-legged birds with back-curved beaks.

"They are firebirds," Laura said. "Their plumage glows like orange coals. There are hundreds of them in the marshes. They seem so wise and saintly. If you told them about the Gospel, they would listen."

Jamie considered for a moment the possibility of preaching to the flamingos. His anxiety had returned; oddly, for a few minutes he had forgotten it. "I'll be going along now," he said. "I'll see you at supper."

"Oh, don't go," Laura said. She patted the seat beside her. "Sit down and watch with me."

Jamie was dubious, but when she patted the seat again he sat down. Laura returned her gaze to a painting on the wall. Jamie was astonished at how little flesh her face carried; her eyes were deep in their sockets and her jaws prominent beneath taut, sallow skin. Yet there was no further question of leaving. He saw that she liked him, esteemed him, inexplicably possessed a perfect affection for him.

He turned his gaze to the painting she watched. The huge painting, in a style that Jamie could recognize only as being very old, was entitled *Trinity*. God the Father, standing, held in his arms the limp, dangling body of the crucified Son. Over them hovered the Dove, encircled by a nimbus of glory. Above all, at the top of the painting, was an equilateral triangle: three yet one. The Father was a man of heroic proportions, bearded, thick haired, grey; his robe and tunic were lavender and brown; rancorless grief filled his face. The body of Christ was nude except for a loincloth. His flesh was the color of ivory; blood spotted his forehead where he had worn a crown of thorns; his hands and feet gaped with the wounds of nails; a crimson gore ran from his pierced side. Like a satin cloth soiled with blood, his body draped, wrinkled and askew, from the arms of the Father.

Choked with pity, Jamie turned to Laura to see how she bore the sight of this sacrificed innocence. Her face was composed, radiant, regal. "As Thou wilt," she murmured.

Looking at Jamie with bland, assured eyes, she said, "Your real name is Joseph."

"No," he remonstrated, "it is Jamie Bolander."

"I won't mention it again," she said. "You may kiss me if you wish, but you may not make love to me. No man can do that. I will always be a virgin."

Her eyes lingered on his until, coerced, he mumbled, "I understand."

"My name is Mary, you know."

"No," he said, "I do not know that. I think it is Laura."

"At least we have found each other again, haven't we?" she said. "You can't always tell just by looking at a person." In a moment she said proudly, "I am large with child. Here, feel me." She unbuttoned her coat. Beneath it she wore what appeared to be a white hospital gown; on its hem was a spot of blood.

"Feel me," she insisted. She took Jamie's hand and laid it on her belly. "It is the Lord Jesus—our Savior." She looked at him quizzically, as if she suspected him of doubt. "No man did it. I am pregnant by the Father."

Pressing Jamie's hand, she asked again, "Do you feel him?"

Jamie's fingers flexed in the softness of her belly; they yearned to feel the Lord. His hunger overbrimmed, and though he knew it was a drama of shadows into which this insane woman sought to project him, he could not say no. "I feel him," he murmured.

Laura was pleased. Tension went from her body and she lifted Jamie's hand and kissed it. "I must be brave," she said. "He is to be crucified a second time. He was to return in glory through me, but the time is not ripe." Her eyes raised again to the painting. "As Thou wilt," she whispered.

Jamie stared at the spot of blood on the hem of her white gown. It was possible that she had been struck by a car and taken to a hospital from which, delirious, she had escaped, all in the brief hours since he had seen her at breakfast.

"You have been hurt," he said.

Laura tugged the flaps of her coat together and with deliberate fingers latched its buttons until once again its collar was snug under her chin. "It's you who have been hurt," she said. "What did they do to you?"

The words stung Jamie and threatened his reserve. "Nothing has happened to me," he lied. "I'm just another missionary doing his duty. A person doesn't have much success, as you said, but it's no worse for me than for anyone else."

"You are grieving," she said. "You have been naked, and no one clothed you, and you have been sick and in prison, and no one visited you."

Unable to restrain himself, Jamie told her everything. His mission was in ruin. How could he preach the gospel of repentance, knowing that he desired men? How could he concentrate on the thousand improvements by which a Christian achieved exaltation when his mind ran so obsessively over the terrain of this single great defect? At first he had prayed with a colossal ardor that God would perform surgery upon his unnatural lust, in return for which Jamie promised to carry out a monumental penance, to undertake some inconceivable regime of self-denial. But his affliction only grew. During the final weeks in Brussels his nights had been filled with horror. When he awoke from his fitful sleep he remembered rank, lush dreams and his heart palpitated with fresh desire. Lying beside his sleeping companion in the cramped bed they shared, he was forced to fight against a despicable impulse to touch and caress him. He saw more clearly every day that this putrescence was part of his true and essential self, that it had been with him from the beginning of his life.

"Precious Joseph, they have hurt you so much," Laura said, her eyes welling with the deepest pity. She pulled him toward her, leaned her cheek against his, and whispered, "My son, if he had lived, would have healed you."

Jamie wept. It was a final compounding of his tragedy to have stumbled into this mad staging of the holy story. He was insatiably hungry for Laura's deception, incurably eager for the salvation she believed in.

"God has given me to the lions. I have been sacrificed," he said.

Laura pulled away from him, her head shaking, her eyes widening. "God will not betray you."

"From the beginning he put me in the track of destructon. I did not ask to love men."

"That is not true," Laura said. "God will sustain you."

"I can't bear the burden. I am crushed."

"Does it hurt so bad?"

"When I find courage, I will kill myself."

A distant, frantic look came into Laura's eyes. She tried to stand but staggered and sat back heavily. She leaned over and opened a satchel which sat at her feet. She removed a rumpled dress, examined it hesitantly, then abruptly stuffed it into the satchel.

"You are the elder who came in from Belgium yesterday," she

said, as if she had only now noticed him for the first time. "I have forgotten your name."

"Jamie Bolander," he reminded her. He sought to speak with casual indifference, though he suffered from a sense of cruel disillusionment. Without warning, the actors and props had been removed from the stage on which he stood. He loathed himself for his gullibility. He had confided his grief to a person who did not exist. He had made himself more vulnerable, had reinforced his despair, had augmented the probability of his self-destruction.

"They say you are going to Lausanne. You will like Switzerland. I was at Geneva first." As Laura spoke, Jamie saw that she suffered. Her face had become dull; her eyelids drooped; her lips strained into a grimace.

"Shall I help you?" he asked.

She pushed away his hand. "The amazing thing about the Midi was the flamingos. Who would ever have guessed there would be wild flamingos there? Once I sat on the bank of a lagoon and I read to the flamingos from the Book of Mormon. Now I dream that I am flying away with them. From high above I see the entire earth—the farms, the fields, the cities, the trains like toys on tiny tracks below me."

"We could go back to the mission home together."

"No," she said, "you go on. I'll rest for a minute. Then I'll be on my way. I'll see you at supper."

"I can't leave you. You are very sick."

"No, I am fine." She struggled to her feet and clutched Jamie's arm to balance herself. "I have been to the clinic of Dr. Telpin in Rue de Chimeux. He wanted me to stay the night, but I found my clothes and left."

"Let's go to the mission home. I will help you."

"I have been voided of a fetus," she said abruptly.

"An abortion!" Jamie said hoarsely.

"I have simply been voided of a fetus," she said insistently. "A fetus has no life independent of the mother."

"What will you do?"

"I will go back to the mission home and tell the president I am ready for a new assignment. Everything will be all right."

"You will be excommunicated."

She shook her head. "I have told no one." She reached for Jamie's hand, bent his fingers into a fist, and brought the fist to her lips. With a kissing sound, she sucked a draft of air through the crevice of the fist. "The operation is very simple. The doctor inserts a long tube and applies a little suction."

Tears streamed down Jamie's cheeks. "The poor innocent," he said. "He never had a chance."

Laura slapped his face with stinging force. Her eyes were fierce with resentment. "This is my affair," she said brutally.

Jamie rubbed his cheek and pulled a handkerchief from his pocket to wipe his eyes. In the distance, through the wide double doors and across the adjoining hall, he saw the grey blank of the misting afternoon against the high arched pane of a window. He turned and said, "I'll be going now."

Laura grasped his arm. He turned back to see a shimmering in her eyes, then tears trickling down her cheeks, then a terrible collapse.

"My baby is dead," she sobbed. "I have killed him."

He opened his arms, let her in, did not resist her fervent grasp. He marveled at the torrential energy of her weeping and could think of no words to console her. Looking up, he found himself gazing on the painting of the Trinity. The dulled sheen of its oils hinted at its venerable age. The figures of the upright Father and of the Son, collapsed in the Father's arms, were larger than actual men. In the forward sky the brilliant Dove radiated streams of glory. The dangling limbs of the Son were more than inert; they were palpably vacant, bearing the unmistakable imprint of a departed vitality. Holding in his tender grasp the bloodied, ivory corpse, the Father received the Son not in glory but in death. A flame of understanding flared in Jamie's mind; his body warmed with a piercing recognition. On the face of the Father there was no rancor, no threat, no vengeance. A colossal grief, galaxies wide, was wrung out upon the brow and cheeks of the very Father, the Sovereign of Infinity, the Everlasting. God the Father, God the Son, God the Holy Ghost. God the Sufferer. An unfamiliar comfort formed in Jamie's heart. In the root of things, the suffering of the innocent was demanded, but at least they wept together, the three of them: Joseph, Mary, and the Father.

Road to Damascus

One Saturday Paul was wakened by the earnest chirruping of birds. The silver-black night still filled the windowpane, and for the thousandth time he asked himself how the birds knew dawn was near. Regina lay at his side, breathing with a tranquil rhythm. Paul, who had gone to sleep in a state of indecision, was pleased now to find himself more resolute. Though Regina would disapprove, he was determined to pay an overnight visit to Sam in the mountains.

Bad news had come from the mines. Christopher, Sam's partner, had disappeared in a subterranean crevice; it was assumed he had fallen to his death. Attracted by the silver strike at Brunhild, Sam had returned to Utah a little over a year ago, bringing Christopher with him. Paul could not grieve for the young man, having seen him only on rare visits to Sam's claim, but the news had left Paul with a renewed anxiety for Sam. In the old days Paul and Sam had drifted from mine to mine and mill to mill. They had worked hard, quit often, spent their cash prodigiously, laughed and gamed and drunk. Like twins, they had been always together until, on a trip into Utah, Paul had met Regina.

Paul dressed and crossed the room, pausing by the dresser near the door. For a moment he was immobilized by shame. Without the slightest premeditation he had made a further decision: he would take money to Sam. At the back of one drawer, tied in a knotted rag, were gold coins—six of them, amounting to eighty dollars. The money was for the new house Paul was building. He lamented the tiny, cramped house, built of unpainted planks, in which his three sons and his little daughter were growing up. Over the years he had brought rock from a quarry, had hammered and broken and chiseled, and one by one had heaped up the finished stones with which, having at last dug the footings, he had lately started the walls of the new house. He could trade cows for rafters and exchange his own labor for plastering. The eighty dollars were for manufactured materials: paint, window glass, brass hinges, and doorknobs with lock and key. Regina hoped there would be a surplus to put toward a stove with enameled panels and an isinglass window, or a carved oak table and a decorative lamp to set upon it. Despite himself, Paul stretched his hand into the drawer and groped among stockings and chemises. He suffered a momentary fancy that the knotted rag might cry out and waken Regina, but she did not stir as he withdrew the tiny bundle and stuffed it into his pocket.

Paul crossed his farmyard. He entered the corral, milked his cow, and returned the bucket, half-filled with warm, foaming milk, to the kitchen. Coming out again, he saw the night waning over the looming wall of eastern mountains. He saddled a horse and placed a packframe on a mule. He went to the garden, and in the growing light he dug new potatoes, carrots, and onions; he picked green corn and from a tree he selected summer apples, which he added to the heaped-up vegetables. Then he saw Regina. She stood at the corner of the saddle shed, pressing her tired face against a grey, warping plank. She had dressed hastily; like a girl, she wore shoes without stockings and a rumpled dress which hung to the midpoint of her calves. Her uncombed hair fell abundantly across her shoulders.

"Was he nice—this boy Christopher that they say is killed?"

Paul shrugged his shoulders. "I hardly knew him. I'm going for Sam's sake."

"It's good of you to take the vegetables and apples to Sam. He will be grateful for them after weeks of johnnycake and sidemeat."

Paul's shame rose. He could not help thinking of the knotted rag bulging in his pocket.

"It will be a pretty day for riding into the mountains," Regina said. The canyon wind, awake at every dawn, sifted her golden hair.

"It will be so," Paul said, waiting warily for her protest. Regina had no capacity for strident talk, yet in her quiet way she was relent-less.

"I saw the milk in the kitchen," she said. "I will milk while you are gone."

"Have Thaddeus do it. He knows how."

"He's only seven."

"My God, I had to plow the fields by the time I was seven!"

Paul unwrapped a lead rope from the hitching post and pulled the mule forward. At the garden he loaded the vegetables and apples in-to the panniers of the packframe. He returned with the mule to the saddle shed and tied an old bedroll over the top of the panniers.

"When will you come home?" Regina asked.

"Tomorrow night."

"We will wait and have Sunday dinner in the evening when you are back. The children won't mind bread and milk at noon."

"Don't wait. I won't be here till late."

Regina stroked the corner plank of the shed, and her eyes fol-lowed the drifting motions of her hand. "Maybe you would rather go on Monday."

"I have hay to put up on Monday," Paul said, scrutinizing her face for malice. "You are afraid of Sabbath-breaking," he said with sud-den disgust. "You think the sky will fall in on Sabbath-breakers."

"It will be an empty table without you," Regina said, seeming not to notice his anger. "The children will wish you were home."

"I don't hear that kind of talk when I go overnight for wood," Paul said derisively. Taking into hand the lead rope of the mule, Paul mounted the horse and, with a dig of his heels, put it into motion.

Regina stepped to the edge of the path and the horse halted. Paul looked down into her face—full cheeks, blue eyes that pleaded; not beautiful, but compelling. He saw intense longing there, longing for him, and sadness too, like the grieving rustle of walnut leaves. Paul could not entirely explain why, years ago, he had been seized by the impulse to abandon Sam and marry Regina. Perhaps he had already begun to feel his age. Or it might have been that Regina seemed un-fortunate and needy. She was quiet and unassertive and suffered an obvious chagrin at approaching thirty without having found a husband. On the day they married, Regina wept. Paul had refused the church, had said no to her faith. It was not easy on a man to find his bride sobbing behind the buggy an hour after the wedding ceremony, yet Paul had hardened his heart. That night, as he made love to her for the first time, her grief roused him to a rushing, willful pleasure.

From behind her back Regina drew a small parcel wrapped in a white cloth. "A lunch," she said, "since I knew you would have to go."

Paul took the lunch. Touched, he searched for words to thank her for the unmerited gift. Regina fingered a strap dangling from the saddle. Suddenly her face brightened.

"Could I ride with you to the edge of the fields?"

Paul looked doubtful.

"The children are asleep," she said. "I'll be back before half an hour."

Paul removed his foot from the stirrup. Regina pulled up her skirt, grasped the cantle and horn of the saddle, and swung into place behind him. Paul kicked the horse forward and turned into the lane. Regina put her arms around him and leaned her face against his back. As the horse plodded along, she chatted cheerfully, as if there were no contention between them.

"One of our hens is brooding," she said. "There are eleven eggs under her. The feathers are gone from her neck, and she sits so solemnly, with her skinny red neck craning this way and that, that I think she must be a cousin of Sister Hacher. Have you seen how long Sister Hacher's neck is? And how she jerks her head about as she peers through her large round spectacles?"

A cottontail rabbit suddenly darted from beneath a bush, leaped the ditch, and dashed into a corn patch. "Come back and be useful," Regina called. "I could use your tail as a sop."

A rip-gut fence, constructed of juniper posts criss-crossed obliquely against one another, lined the lane. "Look at your fields," Regina said proudly. "Each year you add to our cultivated ground. Pretty soon there will be money left over after the mortgage payment is made. Then we won't be so pinched."

On either side of the lane the land bore testimony to Paul's labor.

On the right were alfalfa and corn; on the left, watermelons, sorghum, and wheat. The alfalfa stretched across broad acres, thick and green, rippled by the morning wind into slow waves. Along deep rows, the corn grew into a great entangled thicket of stalks, blades, and tassels. With his draft horses Paul had plowed, harrowed, and furrowed. With a heavy bag he walked the fields in the windy spring and sowed his grain. He thrust seed corn into the ground with a sharp-nosed planter. He went at night as often as in day to take his turn at the irrigation water from the canals, laboring wordlessly for uninterrupted hours, bending his back, straining his arms, lifting out mud with his shovel, filling here and excavating there until his land had slaked its thirst. Weren't these fields a reason for Paul to think well of himself? He sought to answer the accuser in his mind, for the warm clasp of Regina's arms reminded him of the ways in which he disappointed her. Why should he take a poor view of himself? Wasn't he a good provider? And wasn't he a good enough father? "Hold me," little Amy would say, and he would heft her into the air, saying, "Will do so, sparrow," and then he would squeeze her little bare feet and put her onto the wagon to go with him wherever it was he had to go.

The horse had carried them to the foothills. He stopped the animal and Regina slid to the ground. She stood close, seeming to be busy brushing dust from the cuff of his pants. Her face was downcast.

"When you go off to the mines," she said, "I don't sleep. Your empty place in the bed talks to me, and I think that when I see you again you will be dead and they will be carrying you in a tarp."

"I'll be back alive," Paul said.

"I prayed God would bless you."

"I can take care of myself," Paul asserted.

He was moved nonetheless, and he dismounted and stood by her side. They looked back toward a distant western border of jutting mountains. Little towns, scattered houses, quilt-patterned fields, and tree-lined roads filled the valley's stretching miles. A cow bellowed distantly. The wind stirred the branches of a nearby cottonwood.

"I think the wind is God's breath, it seems so sweet and cool," Regina said.

It was sometimes Regina's way to speak whimsically. When they were first married she continued to talk to Paul as a missionary might talk. She tried to tell him about Joseph Smith, about the restored church, about the necessity of baptism by one having true authority. He had blustered and refused to listen. These days Regina spoke obliquely and half in jest.

"God's gold," she said quietly, pointing to the valley.

The valley was divided between night and day—upon its near floor were the blue shadows of the towering eastern mountains, and beyond, upon its western reaches, the drench of the new sun. The mountains in the west stood sharp and clear, their rocks and cliffs and slopes of pinyon and oak incandescent with early light.

God's gold! Paul was reluctant to admit that at times Regina's whimsy reached him. He had his weakness; he could not always be on guard. The kindness she had shown by making his lunch, the sweet hug of her arms as they had ridden through the lane, remained with him. Oddly, it seemed in this instant that the burgeoning beauty of the morning was Regina's gift; it was as if she had called forth a special good cheer, a promise of extraordinary fortune, to accompany him as he rode into the mountains. In such a moment he might almost wish for faith. Sometimes Regina caressed his neck, kissed his forehead, and looked upon him with her bright face, her brows lifted musingly, her glance a caress of health and peace. Her soft hands and tranquil eyes tempted him, quickened his longing, roused him to believe, if only for an instant, that somewhere was an everlasting home. It was far away, but surely somewhere, beyond the western mountains and then again beyond those mysterious purple peaks so far beyond them, was a golden kingdom. Bright with unending sunshine and filled with utter joy, it was the place where God was.

Regina said good-by and walked quickly into the lane. Paul turned to the mule and tightened the cinch on the packframe. Remounting his horse, he watched until his wife's figure had diminished in the distance. He urged his animals on toward the mountains which rose abruptly before him, a gigantic, convolute wall of plunging canyons, crested ridges, and sharp, rocky peaks. Paul had begun already to mistrust his warm feelings for the valley and his farm and Regina. If a man had faith, what became of him? What kind of box did such a man nail himself into? What cords bound his wrists and ankles? This God, who Regina said had spread life and love across the universe, this same God, as Paul had often reminded her, gave commandments to which there was no end. On a frontal ridge were two trees which Paul sometimes contemplated as he shoveled mud to stem a flow of irrigation water or as he worked a slab of rock with mallet and chisel. One of the trees on that high ridge was tall, straight, and conical; the other was curiously warped at midtrunk into a contorted bush. The crippled tree troubled him. It seemed cruelly deflected, thwarted in its movement toward the open sky. The commandments overweighted a man, bent him low, squeezed him into odd shapes like a gnarled, missprouted tree.

Paul entered a canyon. Its massive slopes were lacerated by gullies, ravines, and lateral canyons. Forests of oak, fir, and aspen grew upon its sides. The trail led generally along the bottom, frequently paralleling it some yards above, though at times leaving it for hundreds of yards and zigzagging back and forth over the steep face. It was a faint trail, rarely traveled, slowly being reclaimed by the canyon. It would lead eventually to Brunhild, the bustling mining camp located over the crest and some distance down the other slope of the range; but first it would bring him to the high terrace where Sam worked his tiny mine, a mile or two above Brunhild. At the thought of Sam, Paul's anticipation rose. There would be thick tobacco smoke and the odor of frying sidemeat in Sam's cabin; there would be talk about the old days, about places they had been, women they had known, golden opportunities they had almost grasped. Paul felt suddenly free. Glimpses of the valley, far below, told him how high he had come. He had cast off his impediments. He possessed the floating power of an eagle; he felt the unweighted swing of a diving hawk.

In the late morning Paul stopped at a small meadow. Heat rose from the tall grass and trifling breezes came from one moment to another, mingling odors of hot, resinous gums and dark, shaded mosses. Paul loosened the cinches on his animals, hobbled them, and left them busily cropping grass. He took the bundle in which

Regina had packed his lunch and crossed the creek. He sat leaning against a fir tree and untied the bundle. Wrapped in brown papers were a currant tart and two sandwiches thick with bacon and garden lettuce. His eye fell on a rectangular object, also wrapped in brown paper. It was a book: Regina's Book of Mormon! Disgust and anger surged across his face. He had an impulse to throw it into the trees, or to rip it apart and cast its pages into the creek. He rewrapped the book and for some quaint reason, perhaps no more than that Regina would ask for money to buy another copy if this one should be lost, he crossed the creek and placed it in his saddlebag. Returning to his lunch, he was overcome by incredulity. What could Regina have expected? Did she suppose he would feel coerced to read the book in these free, untrammeled mountains? Or did she think of it as a reminder and a companion, something like a silent, observant bishop riding along at Paul's side to wag a finger or to purse his lips with disapproval? Paul ate the sandwiches and tart, but he could not relish them. He was right to be wary of Regina. She was not so compliant and generous as she sometimes seemed.

Afterward Paul lay in the shade, listening to the crunching and cropping of his animals and to the clear rattling of the little stream where, at the meadow's end, it began another hurried descent over rocks and roots. For a while he could not relax. The day had become strange. He felt as if he were being watched. He sat up once or twice and peered this way and that, but he could see nothing unusual. Finally he dozed. When he awoke, he lay with his eyes closed. Memories coalesced in his mind, hovered strangely, and evaporated. He became aware that, though it was scarcely past noon, the day was cooler and a wind was rising. The boughs of the fir tree overhead fretted and scraped.

The revolving rasp of a wagon filled his memory. Jimmy, his brother, came in the cabin door. "The horses are harnessed," he said.

Their mother put on her bonnet and walked to the door. "Somebody going with me?" she asked.

"I'm going to find the honey tree," Paul's father said.

"Might be other days for doing it," his mother said.

"Might be," his father replied.

"Ain't twice a year the preacher comes, and you got to hunt bees."

Paul's father turned in his chair and began to tie his boot laces.

"You live in these dark woods, and your own boys ain't Christian." Her voice was belligerent, but futility caused her gaunt, seamed face to droop.

The woods were not dark for Paul's father. In the cabin and in the cleared fields of his Ohio farm he was likely to be harsh with his sons and sullen to his wife, but in the woods or along the creeks, following a hound, hunting a deer, or taking catfish, he was another man. If his boys were along, he sang them songs that told sad stories, and he told them how it had been in the army of Ulysses S. Grant.

Paul's mother went out and climbed into the wagon; she clucked and the horses moved forward. Suddenly Paul ran from the cabin. "Wait, Ma!" he shouted.

Paul got to his feet and moved from the fir tree. He knelt at the creek and had a drink. The sky darkened; a chill gathered; a wind swirled, moaning and crooning across the forested slopes. Paul felt an inexplicable anxiety. For no particular reason he gazed through the trees at the far side of the meadow. Suddenly his hair prickled with horror: a tall, thin figure came through the trees. Paul retreated and looked about to see where he might run. Out of the aspens into the meadow, drifting rather than walking, blown like a scuttling leaf in autumn, came a woman. She moved in the folds of a long robe, and her mouth was bound by a cerement, like one prepared for burial.

"Regina!" Paul exclaimed, staring transfixed with horror and licking his lips with a dry tongue.

At the stream she stopped. Though she had passed between the horse and the mule, they made no response to her presence. The dust of time filled the lines of her face. Her grey hair rippled in the wind. She stared past Paul, her features displaying a stark and singular indifference. No rancor showed in her eyes, no hint of malice, harm, or evil, no passion, appetite, or desire, no grief or envy.

"She's dead," Paul said, his face contorting with remorse. "Is it true, Regina? Are you really gone?"

Only the wind sounded. It passed through a hundred thousand

trees with a billowing roar.

"She is dead," he said with finality. Her throat tightened; his breath rasped. For an instant he feared that he, too, was at the brink of the final abyss.

And then, in the blinking of an eye, she was gone.

"No," Paul shouted, "don't leave me!" He ran forward and splashed into the creek. "Don't leave me! Regina! Regina!" His cry was snatched up by the rushing wind and carried across the swaying forest. A sullen rumble answered. He threw back his head and looked into the sky. Dark clouds spilled over the edge of the canyon. Paul looked around. His two animals stood in the meadow, their heads high, their ears pointed alertly toward him.

"Did you see her?" he asked. Then he felt ashamed. Talking to animals! "I'm getting daft," he muttered. He saw that he still stood ankle deep in the flowing water of the creek.

Drops of rain spattered on Paul's head. He trudged to his horse and took a poncho from the saddlebag. A heavy foreboding had filled his heart. Surely a terrible disaster had struck his home. Regina was dead; the children were paralyzed, bewildered, wondering where to go for help. Then it occurred to Paul that the apparition might be nothing more than a dream. Wasn't it conceivable that, by some quirk of indigestion, the sleeping mind of a man might project its dark phantoms into his time of waking? Perhaps Paul had only supposed himself to be awake. Paul could no longer be sure that he had seen Regina's face; it might have been the face of his mother.

Paul rode through the rain in a depressed and sullen mood. In midafternoon he arrived at Sam's cabin, which was silent and cold; undoubtedly Sam was at Brunhild. Paul unloaded the panniers from the mule and placed them in the cabin, then released the mule in a small corral. Paul remounted his horse and, urging it into a trot, resumed his course along the trail. In a moment he passed by a small, dark lake. A moment more brought him by the tailings of Sam's mine. A windlass with a handcrank and metal cogs stood in wooden tripods over the vertical shaft. Paul could not repress the gloomy thought that somewhere beneath his feet, perhaps only a few hundred yards into the earth, Christopher had died.

It was early evening when Paul rode into Brunhild. The single street of the mining camp was crowded with wagons, horses, and sauntering men. On either side jostling rows of false-fronted frame structures gave shelter to stores, banks, assay offices, hotels, and saloons. Paul found Sam in a saloon called Katie's Clippership. He was a tall man with broad, muscular shoulders. A jubilant laugh broke through his grizzled beard, and he gripped Paul's arms with immense bear-paw hands. He made room for Paul at the bar and introduced him to two young men, Raymond and James, who had volunteered in the search for Christopher's body. Katie's Clippership swarmed with drinking, gaming miners. Tobacco smoke curled among glowing kerosene lanterns; the floor was thick with sawdust and mud. A fiddler, mounted on a high stool, scraped at his instrument, scarcely making it heard over the din of laughing voices. Girls clad in scanty costumes and dark fishnet stockings served drinks at the tables. Katie herself, a hoarse, weathered madam, stood smiling at the end of the bar. Occasionally a man would speak to her, and in a moment he would disappear with one of the girls through a door at the back of the hall.

"There's garden truck for you at the cabin—new potatoes, carrots, and onions; sweet corn; apples ready for a pie if you're of a mind to have one," Paul said. "I brought them up on a mule. I left her in your corral."

"Fresh victuals!" Sam exclaimed with pleasure. "I'll show you something about cooking new potatoes. We'll have a Sunday dinner like you haven't tasted in a long time! That's a real favor you did me; vegetables don't sell cheap in these parts."

Sam told Paul about the search for Christopher. The young man had fallen from a catwalk crossing a fissure which interrupted the horizontal shaft of the mine. No one knew why he had fallen or how deep the fissure might be. Secured by a harness, Sam had dangled from a rope, had searched nearby ledges, and had shouted in vain for his lost comrade.

"I've lost my spirit for working that mine," Sam said. "Even before this happened, I had about made up my mind it was finished. The assays show some silver, but it's got to get a lot richer or it isn't worth building a road."

"I wish we could fetch his body out," Raymond said. "God, I keep thinking, what if he's waiting for us to come?"

"Shall I go have a look in the morning?" Paul asked.

"I'll go down with you," Sam said. "But there isn't anything any of us are going to do about it. He's gone."

"Why don't we quit worrying about Christopher?" James said.

"He ain't worrying about anything. Why should we?"

"That's a good idea," Sam said. "Let's think about something else. Maybe I got enough for one more drink." He dug into his pocket, withdrew a few silver coins, and looked at them dubiously. "This is the last of it, boys. But, hell, what's money for?" He motioned to the burly bartender.

Paul sipped his whiskey and listened while Sam told stories. "You recall when we invaded Missoula for the first time?" Sam was saying. "You and me and that scrawny powdermonkey named Georgie Rockwell. Georgie set a wooden powder box down on the bar and an old geezer who hadn't cut his hair in forty years says, Does your box have in it what it says it's got in it? And Georgie sets his lighted cigar down on the box and wipes his nose and says, What the hell else would it have in it? And that old fellow picks up his hat and rolls his eyes to the ceiling and walks out without a word, so Georgie picks up the drink the old fellow hadn't got to touch and finishes it off."

"I remember," Paul said, laughing. Sam's voice was soothing and affectionate, and Paul again felt the old regret for having broken off with him. Paul took the knotted rag from his pocket, untied it, and laid out before Sam the eighty dollars in gold coins.

Sam looked blankly at the coins.

"It's for you. For old times' sake."

Still Sam seemed doubtful. Paul smiled and pushed the coins toward him. For an instant Sam's eyes glistened with moisture. "You haven't forgotten your old pardner," he said in an intense voice. "There never was anybody like Paul."

A girl brushed by with a tray of glasses. Sam turned and gazed wistfully after her. "It wouldn't be right to spend some of it that way, would it?" he said in a tone of resignation.

"You spend it however you want," Paul insisted. "It's yours."

"For all of us, then," Sam said, brightening. "These boys have been damned good to help look for Christopher. And hell, pard, you got your rights to a little fun, too."

"No, I couldn't do that," Paul said quickly.

But Sam had not heard. He signaled Katie, who came along the inner aisle of the bar. "For me and my friends," he said, pushing coins forward.

"Sally's ready," Katie said with a motion of her hand. "Who's first?"

Paul turned from the bar and found himself looking at a pretty brunette. Her mouth formed a bland, friendly smile; her bare arms were white and plump; her half-exposed breasts, pushed upward by her costume, quivered slightly as she rocked on unsteady heels. Paul was seized by a feverish excitement. There was no chaperon, no censor, no judge to deny him. It suddenly seemed that he had been living in a stupor, chained by unexamined assumptions, existing from day to day and year to year within the vows of his marriage for no other reason than that he had not thought of doing otherwise.

Then he heard his own hollow voice, speaking as if from the far end of a vacant hall, saying, "I can't do it, Sam."

"You can't do it!" Sam exclaimed. His mouth was round with surprise. "Sure you can! I know old Paul!"

"I can't, Sam."

An hour later, the four companions jogged their horses along the trail toward Sam's mine. The storm had broken and a high, bright moon blanched the ridges and ravines. A few dark clouds with bronzed, billowing edges drifted in the sky. Before leaving the saloon Sam had bought two bottles of whiskey. One they had placed in Paul's saddlebag; the other they shared as they rode along. After a while James began to sing old ballads. His horse had trotted into the lead, and his melodious tenor echoed from slopes and cliffs. Paul struggled to keep his wits; he knew he was drinking too much on an empty stomach. He was thinking of Regina. She had become frightened of getting pregnant again. She did not trust Paul to withdraw from her at the moment of his climax. Despite herself, she tightened her legs and forced her pelvis against him; ironically, her resistance sometimes roused Paul to a cruel energy and he heedlessly took his full desire. Afterward, while Regina wept quietly by his side in the dark bedroom, he loathed himself. As his horse jogged along the trail, Paul also thought of Sally, the whore in Katie's Clippership, remembering the consenting promise of her smile and the quaking, overbrimming swell of her breasts. His anger mounted. He despised himself for the opportunity he had thrown away.

At a widening of the trail, Sam urged his horse alongside Paul's. "How's things on the farm?"

"Quiet and slow," Paul said. "But pretty at this time of year— the crops are thick and green."

"Do you ever get a yen to quit?"

"It enters my mind," Paul said. "But what would I quit for? My fields are laid out and my irrigation ditches are dug and done."

"I never heard of anybody striking it rich on a farm," Sam said.

"A man can keep food on the table."

"You can't drift on to new diggings."

"That's true. A farm has got you, year in and year out."

"Tied and throwed and ready for the branding iron and castrating knife," Sam said.

"That's strong talk," Paul said. "Have you got something special against farming?"

"Not if my old pard is happy doing it."

"It's been forever since I did something just for the hell of it."

"Remember that time in Durango when we blowed five hundred dollars in a day and a half?"

"It was five hundred for sure," Paul said incredulously. "It seems like something someone else might have done. But I recall it didn't worry me any to do it. On Monday we went over to the mill and hired on and went back to work."

"We used to talk about Alaska," Sam said. "It's still an open place."

"Alaska!" Paul said fervently. "By God, wouldn't that be something? It would be a dream."

"I'd like to see that country," Sam said. "I'm looking for a pardner. Raymond and James are good boys, but they aren't in a mood for the northland."

"I've got four kids."

"You can send them twenty times what you've got now. Money's big and easy to come by in Alaska. Those who told me know what they're talking about."

"We're not so young anymore."

"The question is, What are you going to do with your life while you've got it?" Sam said. "If you're happy dancing to the tune a woman plays, well, have at it. But me—I've still got some life to live. By God, you aren't going to find me rocking on the porch of some old folks' home. When I can't live like a real man, then I'm ready to go under."

They rode silently for a while. James's tenor drifted eerily through the night air.

Paul's face burned. "I'm nothing but a goddamned horse standing thirsty by a gate, waiting for somebody's say-so before I can go down to the creek and have a drink. I'm a piece of property; I'm sectioned off and fenced in; and some son of a bitch has put a mortgage on me."

"There's big doings ahead, Paul. There's fellows we ain't met, sights we ain't seen, meadows full of flowers and green with grass to make you catch your breath, sunsets burning red over mountain ranges that ain't even got a name, women who let you do to them what it is you want to do."

"I'll come! I'm with you!" Paul said passionately. "We'll ride down off these mountains and turn north, and, by Jesus, we won't ever come back to these parts."

Sam laughed. "We'll make tracks for the big country. Paul and Sam! There wasn't ever anybody else like us!"

Paul flung out his arms exuberantly. "I'm going where the geese go," he shouted. "I'm flying loose and free! Give me room!" He dug his heels into the ribs of his horse, and the animal spurted into a run.

"Waahoo for Alaska!" Sam shouted as he whipped up his horse. The two friends clattered up the moonlit trail while the cliffs resounded with the wild clamor of their delight.

On Sunday morning, the four went to the mouth of the mine. The long, deep bucket held only one person, and Paul went first, dangling by a cable spun off the hand-operated windlass. The bucket clanked and banged against the walls, filling his ears with dismal, twisted reverberations. Fine jets of water sprayed into the shaft. The feeble light of his lantern glinted upon the pasty slime of this gigantic gut of stone.

At the bottom Paul climbed from the bucket, stood aside, and heard it rise clanking above him. Its sound grew fainter and fainter until only a weak drumming pervaded the fetid air. Paul was to wait for Sam, but could not force himself to sit quietly. He stooped and labored along the horizontal shaft, until it opened suddenly into a cavern. Paul did not think he had gone far, yet, as he held his lantern forward, he saw before him a gaping fissure skirted precariously by a catwalk of planks.

Paul knelt and held his lantern over the fissure. He peered more intently.

"Christopher!" he shouted.

Echoes converged from a hundred points. "Christopher! Christopher! Christopher!"

Paul edged back. He set the lantern by his side and groped for a rock. In coming about again, he tumbled the lantern over; desperate, he lunged for it, but it was gone. He watched with a horrified stare until it struck far below and went out. He listened for what seemed a long time to its faint echoing clatter.

Paul drew himself gingerly back from the void, found the damp wall of the cavern, and sat against it. He thrust his hand before his face. He tried to see it. He compelled himself; he willed vision with a desperate surge of energy. But everywhere was absolute, unyielding darkness. And then it seemed, right at his side, something sat! Paul held himself perfectly still. He could not risk a motion or even so much as a thought. He heard the faint, distant rush of subterranean waters. And though he at first refused to hear it—he told himself it could not be so—he heard a deep, labored breathing, like the breathing of an asthmatic or a stricken animal.

A cloth brushed his face. The thin, dangling strip smelled of the seepage of a wound and was crusted as if with blood. Paul tore at his face as if it were covered by wasps. His hands found nothing. He saw flames licking hungrily around a great black pot; boiling soap foamed over the lip of the kettle, redoubling the fire. The sun glistened through the haze of Indian summer. The clearing was littered by autumn leaves—red, orange, brown. Some of them hung yet in the maples. Here and there, sifted by the breeze, they relinquished their hold and drifted to the ground.

"No," Paul whimpered. "No, please, no." He started up. Then he remembered the fissure. He wrapped his head in his arms and tried to suffocate the memory.

A voice spoke. "Do you hear me, Paul?"

"Yes," Paul said at last, "I hear you."

His mother came from the house. Paul followed her. She stumbled at the fire. Her scream drowned in the bubbling soap. In a moment she pulled herself from the kettle and ran into the woods. Her shrieks hurtled through the air, one upon another. The doctor wrapped her in thin strips of cloth soaked in boric acid. Paul was asleep early one morning in the corner of the room where she lay. He was awakened by a stir among the big people and he knew she had died.

"I can't stand it!" Paul cried. He rose and started to slide along the wall, but his head whirled dizzily, and he could not remember where the fissure lay. He sank again, his back to the wall.

"Do you know me, Paul?" the voice muttered.

"Who are you?" shouted Paul.

His echo rebounded. "Who are you? Who are you? Who are you?"

The voice said, "Yes. Who am I?"

"I know you."

"You have always known me, haven't you, Paul?" the voice said.

"Yes," Paul said quietly.

"No one escapes me, do they, Paul?"

"No one."

"It will not be long and I will come for you."

Paul's temples pounded; violence and fire possessed his mind. He could not be sure whether he was senseless or awake. Then suddenly there came the clank of metal on rock, the muffled sound of the descending bucket.

When Paul and Sam came up from the mine, they found Raymond alone at the windlass. On the terrace beyond the cabin, at the edge of the little mountain lake, James stood naked, a bottle in one hand and a book in the other.

"He's taking a bath," Raymond said. "He's already hitting that other bottle you bought."

"We better get up there before it's all gone," Sam muttered.

Paul panted heavily on the slope. Sam looked back. "You don't look so good," he said. "Do you feel sick?"

Paul nodded. "I feel pretty bad. It was cold in the mine."

James set the bottle and book on the ground. Clinging to a rock at the edge of the deep lake, he eased himself into the water. He swam a few strokes, then turned back. Shouting and laughing, he pulled himself out, took up a towel made from a flour sack, and rubbed his body dry. The other men sat on a log and watched, warm in the brilliant morning. Drops of water sparkled on delicate white flowers and on pale, drooping mountain grass. A blue jay screamed in a nearby thicket, and a squirrel clattered along the rough bark of a fir.

Sam picked up the bottle, drank, and handed it to Paul. Paul reached for the bottle, then stopped and smiled apologetically. "Maybe I shouldn't."

Sam screwed up his lips and shook his head. "Take a drink," he said. "It'll stoke your stove and burn off the chill of the mine. There isn't any reason why we shouldn't feel good, is there? I got some stories to tell you haven't heard."

Raymond picked up the book from the ground and held it before his friends. "Look, a Mormon Bible!"

Paul stared at the book. "Where did that come from?"

"It was in the saddlebag with that bottle," James said. "Mixing your religion with your fun, ain't you? Or maybe you meant for you and old Sam here to read this Bible while Raymond and me took care of this whiskey. I call that gentlemanly of you."

Paul took the book and leafed through it. He shook his head dismally.

"No need to look so down about it," James said. "I ain't ashamed of it. I'd be glad to have a Bible. If you don't want this one, let me have it."

"It isn't a Bible—not exactly, anyhow. It belongs to my wife. I didn't ask her to send it along. She's always got God on her mind.

She isn't one to take a text and preach a sermon, but I know what she's thinking. She has her ways of talking, even when she isn't saying words."

"Some men ain't afraid to knock their woman down if she needs it," Raymond said.

"It don't make no difference," Sam said. "It's all in the past now. She can't do you any harm."

Paul slumped. He felt extraordinarily fatigued, as if he had been several days without food.

"Put it out of your mind," Sam said. "We got better things to think about."

"I can't put it out of my mind," Paul said. "In any corner of my farm, out in the hayfield, in the milkshed, no matter where, I can't get away from it. The air stinks of the commandments, like a corral full of manure. I know what she's thinking: God wants this and he doesn't want that; cut down on doing one thing and pick up on doing another; wash out your mouth and clean up your mind; keep the Sabbath and pay your tithing. God!"

Paul leaped to his feet. With a violent heave, he threw the book into the air, where it fluttered open and fell with rustling pages into the lake. Stunned silence held the men while the book splashed and circular waves spread from the spot where it struck.

James said, "You shouldn't of done that."

Paul ran to the edge of the lake and dived in, boots, clothes, and all. He was engulfed in snowmelt water. The cold pounded at his body as if with hammers. He flung his arms about, feeling for the book but grasping only water. Down, down, down. Then his hand touched the sacred book. He closed on it, took it firmly, let his feet sink below him to find the bottom and shove himself upward. There was no bottom.

He kicked and stroked, but still he sank. A scalding fear surged through his veins. His lungs convulsed. They asked only one breath of air. To pull and draw again, to suck so easily in and out the animating air! Paul saw himself sitting with a plate of sliced tomatoes and a shaker of salt. The cabin door was open. Specks of dust floated from the darkness of the room into a bright shaft of noonday sun. His mother came from the hearth, her skirt scraping the puncheon floor. She forked a chop onto his plate, then sat by him.

"They say Jimmy drinks," she said. "What'll I do if he goes the way of his pa?"

Paul gazed upon his plate while his mother wept; he saw obliquely the convulsions of her body. Her fatigue lanced his shoulders like a scalpel.

Then his tight-clenched jaws and his retching throat brought him back to the water engulfing his sinking body. Somewhere above, in the water or out, he could not know, half-hidden amid swirling, glistening bubbles of air, a woman came smiling. It was Regina, he thought. She was barefoot and clothed in white, and her golden hair floated in the breeze. Her face was brilliant with a reflected light, and her eyes looked eagerly forward.

It seemed to Paul that he, too, could see the light. It came from that distant kingdom beyond the western mountains where dawn has broken forever and oceans roar a chorus of infinite praise to God, where God Himself sits in blinding robes and utters the word that elevates continents and casts off globules of stellar fire. Paul stroked once more, crying out now to his limbs for a strength they had never before possessed. He felt nothing but the grind of his tight-shut jaws and the flowing force of his arms and legs. The light beckoned, and he stroked to reach it.

In the sky above the bank where they pulled him, while he lay gasping and his face slowly turned from black to red, unseen in its approach came a bird, a mountain mourning dove. It stopped in midair above him, confused, then fluttered and flew away.

When he came to his senses Paul looked about at his companions with shame and uncertainty. He pulled off his boots and drained them of water. Piece by piece he removed his clothes and wrung them out and put them on again.

Finally he nodded at the three men and said, "Thanks."

"You had me scared, pardner," Sam said. "I'd for sure given you up for drowned."

James picked up the dripping book and placed it on the log. "Might be a way of drying it out if you hung it up just right."

Sam squinted ruefully down the slope toward the windlass standing over the mouth of his mine. "After dinner, maybe we ought to ride back to Brunhild and start looking for someone to buy this claim," he said. "To tell the truth, I'm in a mood to clear out of this country fast. If she don't sell easy, you boys can take her for nothing."

"Don't believe we're interested," Raymond said.

"Can't blame you," Sam said. "A washed-out claim ain't a bargain at any price. Well, I can sell the windlass and those tunnel timbers. Maybe the stove in the cabin will bring a little something."

With unsteady legs Paul was walking the path leading past the cabin to the corral. He took a bridle from a post and walked out onto the meadow where his hobbled animals cropped grass among the horses of his friends. He bridled his horse and led him to the saddle hanging from the side of the cabin. Sam followed and stood near the door, watching as Paul threw a blanket onto the horse.

"You got a mind to take a ride?"

"I'm going home," Paul said.

"Got some affairs to settle, I imagine."

"I guess I won't be back."

"You don't mean that, pardner," Sam said. "Your fire's burning low; you had a tough thing happen to you. Come in and rest a little. I'll cook you up a bite to eat."

Sam disappeared through the cabin door. In a moment he reappeared, carrying a coffee pot. He poured a mug and handed it to Paul. Paul took the mug and squatted. He sipped, blew on the surface of the steaming liquid, stared moodily into it, then took a gulping swallow.

"Those were good times we had," Paul said.

Sam squatted beside him. "Yeah. Good times."

"I couldn't ever pretend they didn't happen."

"The good times ain't over yet," Sam said softly.

Paul handed the empty mug to Sam, stood, hefted the saddle and threw it onto the horse's back.

"How long is it we've been friends?" Sam said. "Seems like we were nothing but kids."

Paul pulled the cinch tight and pushed against the horse to test the firmness of the saddle. "Keep the mule," he said. "I wish I had more to give you."

"It ain't a mule I need," Sam said. "I need my friend."

Paul mounted the horse and kicked it in the ribs. The horse snorted and broke into a gallop. Paul reined in the surging animal and pulled about. Shielding his eyes with his hand, he looked toward the looming peaks and forested ridges. "There's nothing like the mountains under a summer sun," he said. Then he gave the horse its head.

Paul rode hard and tried to think only about the lurch and thrust of the saddle. After a couple of hours he came to a high ridge where the trail overlooked the western valley. He paused there and dismounted. A patchwork of fields and pastures spread across the valley. A dusty haze hung over the little towns and along the roads. Ponds and creeks glistened in the afternoon sun. Paul peered closely and there, far below, he could see the blocks of his own farm. On a ridge across the canyon from where he stood were two trees. One was tall and conical, the other bent and bushy. Paul looked for a moment and then, leaning his head against the neck of his horse, he wept bitterly. At last he shook his head, mounted his horse, and rode into the canyon.

The Shriveprice

Darrow's faith had returned to him without warning or solicitation. In his seventieth year he had gone with a friend to St. Louis to attend a World Series game in the splendid new stadium. After the game they had wandered to the giant arch of stainless steel on the bank of the Mississippi. Darrow was captivated. Unbelievably slender, triangular in section, pinned to the earth only at its two bases, the glittering arch was a daring application of geometry against wind and gravity. He had stood with his back to the river, looking westward through the arch, and thought, as he had not thought for a long time, about his own westgone people. It was as simple as that. In an instant, without fanfare or commotion, Darrow believed again.

On a bright morning in Kentucky the summer following the return of his faith, Darrow had watched his son and daughter-in-law play a furious game of tennis. Cecily, his granddaughter, sat on his lap. For a while Darrow responded to the charm of the spreading walnut trees and to the comfort of Cecily, who snuggled in his arms. Grief slowly grew in his mind: there was nothing in Cecily's life to condition her impulses toward salvation; this precious child was growing inevitably into damnation. From that moment, his prayers for absolution became hollow and unconvinced. Though he had been quietly rebaptized into the church, he feared that the recanting of an old man was meaningless. It was not righteousness, but the narrowing opportunities of old age that crowded him from his corruptions. The improvements and perfections for which mortal life was

given were stillborn. His taint defied cleansing; the sinroot had gone
too deep.

Then, near the end of the same summer, a letter came from Leah,
Darrow's sister, inviting him to a reunion of the Sevy family. He accepted, and for the first time in forty-five years he returned to Utah.
Sara, Leah's daughter, met him at the Salt Lake airport and took
him to her apartment in the city. Looking at her smooth, unweath-
ered face, Darrow was startled to realize that she was nearly forty.
She intended to join Darrow at Leah's house in Lehi, but for the
moment she seemed to have forgotten that her purpose in coming to
her apartment was to pack her bag. She sat on the sofa with a high-
heeled shoe propped against the coffee table and talked with wide-
eyed intensity.

"Have you heard of this stupid book of Cousin Claiborne's?"
Sara was saying. "It brings up the whole matter of Joram and
Ruhannah. It's supposed to be a biography of Joram. The manuscript will be presented at the reunion; Claiborne wants the family to
publish it as Great-grandfather's official life story. But what a
travesty! Cousin Claiborne doesn't have a historical bone in his
body. The book is nothing but sentimental mush, folklore, any silly,
pious thing anybody in the Sevy family ever said about Joram. I can
guarantee there will be skirmishes fought over Claiborne's book. A
few of us see it for what it really is, and we don't intend to have it
published without a fight."

"That's a little frightening," Darrow said. "I wouldn't think any
book would be worth fighting over. It can't hurt anybody, can it?"

"Maybe you don't remember Cousin Claiborne very well," Sara
said. "He's typical of a certain personality in the family—pompous,
convinced that God has endorsed his special projects, and absolutely unwilling to let you ever forget that he's a retired vice-president of
Utah Valley Bank. But that is irrelevant. What matters is that I've
read the manuscript, and the book slanders Ruhannah. I knew it
would, but it made me boil all over again to see those things in
writing."

Darrow shifted his eyes from Sara's gaze and looked uncertainly
about the room. He was an appealing man despite his age; his arms
were brown and muscular, his hair silver and profuse. "I knew

Joram," he said, half-abstractedly, as if he spoke to himself. "So did Leah—better than I did, in fact, because she was born five years earlier. Could we be so old, remembering a man who saw the Salt Lake Valley when it was only sagebrush?"

Darrow had heard Ruhannah's story in his youth. Ruhannah claimed that Joram, Darrow's grandfather, had sacrificed a friend, a thing to be understood as an act of blood atonement. The story was attributable to the bitterness of Ruhannah, the second of Joram's five wives, who in her later years had divorced Joram and had apostatized from the church. Darrow was astonished that Ruhannah's accusation was still remembered—that, some hundred and fifteen years after the supposed deed had occurred, the rumor of it was still an issue in the Sevy family. Darrow was also astonished by the sudden revulsion which had swept over him as he listened to his niece. The very idea of blood atonement, this principle of a final desperate purchase of salvation for the guilty through the shedding of their blood, was barbaric. With a tremor of anxiety Darrow noted that, of the possible solutions to the problem of damnation, blood atonement was one he had not yet considered.

"It's obvious that I'm on Ruhannah's side," Sara said.

"Do you have to take sides?"

"If you're in the majority party of the Sevy family, you've got to believe Ruhannah made up her story out of malice."

"I don't remember the family being divided into parties. Isn't it something you'd be just as well off forgetting?"

"It isn't something people will let you forget. There is a gross overrating of Joram, and it's always done at the expense of Ruhannah. You would be disgusted to see how some people have deified Joram—including Mother."

"It seems odd that people should make so much of Joram," Darrow said. "But even if they make too much of him, even then I'm afraid I don't have the heart to believe Joram killed that fellow."

"Which means that you believe Ruhannah lied about him."

Darrow took out a penknife and began to pare a fingernail. "I'd rather not think anything at all about it."

"Joram being a man, you can't believe he would commit a religious murder. But Ruhannah being a woman, you can easily believe she would spread an abominable lie."

"Who knows what really happened in the past?"

"I know that Ruhannah would not have lied."

"You were there? You saw with your own eyes?"

"Yes," Sara said triumphantly, "in a sense I was there. I have a copy of Ruhannah's diary." She rose and disappeared into her bedroom. In a moment she returned and motioned for Darrow to sit close beside her on the sofa. On the coffee table before them she opened out the roughly bound pages of a photocopied document. The original, she explained, had recently come to one of their cousins, a professor of history at BYU, from the family of the woman who had nursed Ruhannah in her last illness. "Claiborne pretends it isn't authentic. But you have only to read it to know that it is."

Darrow bent and scrutinized the tilting, jostling lines of Ruhannah's handwriting.

"She was an intelligent woman," Sara said. "It's a rare journal. Mostly our old pioneer diary-keepers talk about trivialities—about gathering eggs and putting up hay. But Ruhannah had feelings to talk about. What spiritual gifts she had! Here, look at this passage."

I was wakened this erly morning by a loud ratteling at my door. It was Mrs. Johnsen from behind the block. Her husband is in the mines and she had no one else to come to. Her littlest child was screeming in pain. I laid hands upon her and blest her unto recovery. Only shortly and the little thing went off to sleep. I feel to thank the Lord for this kindness.

"That is the woman the Sevy family makes out to be a villainness," Sara said. "There are dozens of passages like that— many of them, like this one, coming long after she is supposed to be living in apostasy and darkness. She was prayerful and good tempered, and she helped her neighbors. Nobody can deny her godliness—except those who are afraid to read her diary. And you wouldn't believe how many of our cousins won't even touch it!"

Twilight was gathering as Darrow and Sara took the southbound freeway for Lehi. Streetlamps and neon lights cast a diffuse glow in

the bronze dusk of the city. As she drove, Sara continued to talk; she
gripped the wheel tightly and repeatedly took her eyes from the
road, directing them to the side where Darrow sat. He struggled to
retain his neutrality, to reassure himself of his indifference to this
old affair between Joram and Ruhannah. He puzzled over Sara's
obvious attempt to make a convert of him. He feared her zeal and
her air of authority, although he could not fail to admire the precise
competence of her personality and the knowing polish of her
body—crisp pants and blouse, dark penciling about her eyes, hair
with sheen and curl. It disturbed Darrow to suppose that a significant minority of the family shared her passion for discrediting
Joram. Was it simply an attempt to elevate Ruhannah, to rectify a
perceived injustice to this one woman? Or did it imply a congenital
dissent within the family, an infusion of a deviant gene among the
Sevy cousins, a deep, shadowy kindred of perversity? Suddenly he
cared immensely whether Joram had committed the bloody deed of
which Ruhannah had accused him. There had been Sevys before
Joram, but Darrow knew little about them. Wasn't Joram the
founder of his line? Hadn't he been a pioneer? If Joram had carried
a condemning guilt to Judgment, what hope was there for a lesser
man like Darrow?

The next morning Leah served Darrow and Sara gooseberry pancakes for breakfast. The table in her small kitchen was covered by a
bright yellow cloth and set with gleaming dishes. Leah bustled between the stove and table, providing her brother and daughter with
flat, steaming cakes. At last she brought a stack to her own plate and
sat down. She wore a simple gingham dress on her diminished
frame, and above her thin, bony face she had arranged her grey hair
into a hemisphere of tight, tiny curls. Her brown eyes sparkled, and
her voice rose in animation as she alternately complained and
boasted about a surfeit of vegetables from her garden, the dying
Lombardy poplars along her fence, and her recent success in ridding
her sewer line of roots.

Sara intended to ride horses with a friend in American Fork and
was dressed in jeans and boots. During the meal she scarcely looked
at her mother. Having finished her pancakes, she sat drumming her
fingers lightly on the table. At a lull in Leah's talk Sara leaned

toward Darrow and said, "When I get back from riding, I want to show you a passage in Joram's journal."

For a moment the eyes of the two women locked. Disappointment crossed Leah's face, and then a bristling anger. "So you are already into that?" she said bitterly.

"It appears that Mother will not let me take her copy of the journal," Sara said. "I will have to show you some other time."

"Won't let you take it!" Leah snorted. "You can look in Grandfather's journal anytime you want. And a lot of good it will do you! There's nothing to see. Those who want contentions know how to make them out of thin air."

"Joram was in Salt Lake City on the weekend of September 21, 1856," Sara said. "He could easily have heard Brigham Young's sermon on blood atonement."

"That statement has to be corrected," Leah said. "Grandfather took calves to the city on September 18—a Thursday. That's all the journal says."

Sara wiped her mouth with her napkin and pushed back her chair.

"Go ahead and tell him," Leah said. "You'll get around to it sooner or later. I just as well hear what invention you've come up with this time."

"It isn't an invention that makes people defensive," Sara said dryly. "It's the truth that hurts."

"Just go ahead," Leah fumed. "Get it over with."

"I will," Sara said, pulling her chair close to the table. Evading her mother's eyes, she went on in an emphatic, slightly elevated voice. Joram's journal, under the heading of November 6, 1856, recorded the burial at Joram's West Canyon ranch of S. Johanssen, who, the journal stated, had died of a gunshot. The journal entry had to be viewed in the context of the Mormon Reformation of 1856. Though the Saints had been on the Utah frontier for only nine years, there were fire-eating apostles who preached that the Saints had grown too prosperous and complacent. Picking up their theme, Brigham Young had preached his famous sermon. To Darrow's surprise, Sara had memorized phrases from it: "There are sins," she quoted, "for which men, if they had their eyes open to their true condition, would be perfectly willing to have their own blood spilt upon the ground, that the smoke thereof might ascend to heaven as an offering for their sins." The entry in Joram's journal about the death of Johanssen, coming as it did within six weeks of Brigham Young's sermon, coupled with Ruhannah's later accusation, made Joram's guilt inevitable. Sara granted extenuations for Joram. Undoubtedly he had been in a nearly hysterical state of mind owing to the isolation of the West Canyon ranch and to the terrible losses he had suffered during the persecutions in Missouri and Illinois and during the exodus to the Rocky Mountains. Probably Johanssen himself, motivated by a devastating guilt, had requested his own execution, making Joram a participant in a holy suicide. Regardless, Sara was certain that none other than Joram had pulled the trigger of the gun that killed Johanssen.

While Sara talked, Leah shifted restlessly in her chair and, with a vindictive fork, pushed a morsel of pancake to and fro across her plate. When Sara had finished and looked expectantly toward her mother, Leah diverted her eyes and seemed to scrutinize the joint where the wall of the kitchen met the ceiling. Sara turned back to Darrow and said, "Don't you agree that there is more here than mere coincidence?"

"I don't know what to think," he said helplessly. "Please don't draw me into it."

"I don't have to tell you that you won't find any of this in Claiborne's book. At least you know the other side of the story now." With that, Sara stood and left the room. After a moment Darrow heard her leave the house, start her car, and drive away.

"She said all of that for my benefit," Leah said. "She'll bait me anytime she thinks she can get me to explode. But I've got smart lately. I refuse to give her the satisfaction."

"What a terrible thing!" Darrow said.

"Yes, imagine her trying to proselyte you in my own kitchen! She has a black tongue, that girl has."

"I don't know what to believe."

"Sara makes it seem so plausible," Leah said, "but I think it's my turn to say a few things now. It won't take long to set the record straight. Wouldn't Grandfather have mentioned Brigham Young's sermon if he had heard it—considering that Brigham was the prophet and president of the church? And what if Grandfather *had* heard it? That wouldn't mean a thing. Blood atonement was never practiced by anyone in the church. It wasn't even thought of. Everyone who heard Brigham Young knew what he meant: if you murder someone, the law will execute you. But all those other wild things about blood atonement—they are the invention of Gentiles and apostates.''

"Sara seems to have every confidence in her story."

"If Sara isn't careful, she'll end her days as an apostate," Leah said grimly. "Things have got worse in late years, Darrow. All the laxness and immorality of the world—it's got in among the Saints, you know. Honestly, I sometimes think Sara is a person I never knew in all my life. She's even into this ERA thing. What do women want nowadays? I don't want to be a man. Why do they?''

Later Leah drove Darrow along the streets of Lehi, where they reviewed remnants of their childhood—the spot where Joram's house had stood, now part of a high school playing field; other fine old yellow brick houses with multiple gables, still owned by families of pioneer vintage; Gardiner's Mercantile, incongruously perched between new buildings housing a bank and a franchise shoe store; the third ward chapel, vacant and unused.

At midmorning Darrow strolled with Leah along the graveled pathways of the Lehi cemetery. Cool evaporation rising from the damp carpet of grass tempered the heat of the bright summer sun. Darrow saw, as he and Leah passed among the ranks and rows of stones, that the town he had once known was gathered in this cemetery. At every other step he came upon a name, engraved in granite or marble, that moved him with affection or grief. Darrow paused before the stone of Jacob Benton, a retarded mute whose sister Doris had dressed him every morning in clean bib overalls and had sent him to spend the day in Gilbert's Drugstore on Main Street. On every weekday for uncounted years, Jake Benton had occupied the same stool at the drugstore counter from nine to twelve and from one to five. He sat, hunched and sagging, saying nothing, drooling a little, staring with wide, innocent eyes at everyone who entered.

"Reginald Gilbert gave that stool to Jake," Darrow said. "It was Reginald's contribution to the mentally handicapped. And, you know, nobody minded old Jake at all."

"Of course people minded!" Leah protested. "Doris should have kept him out of sight."

Darrow squatted by the grave. "Old Jake!" he said reverently. "So even you had to die?"

A little later he paused before another stone. It marked the grave of Timothy Crofter, a boy whose skull had been crushed by a horse's kick. "When I heard about the accident, I ran down to the livery barn on First East," Darrow explained. "They had already taken his body away. I remember squatting on the sidewalk, looking at his trampled hat and at a little blood that had puddled in the dust. The next day in school it seemed odd to see his empty desk."

"God has his reasons for calling children home," Leah said. "It's very sad for us who stay behind, but it's better for them."

They strolled on. Darrow stopped before the stone of Karl Bjorlund. "Here's one who suffered," he said. "He had cancer of the face. His brothers kept him locked in a room so that he wouldn't kill himself. He took a stick of firewood and tried to beat himself to death with it. I don't know how long it took him to die."

In time they came to the graves of their father and mother, John and Nellie Parker Sevy. "Look at this weed," Leah said, stooping to pull a plant growing on their mother's grave.

Darrow turned half away and looked toward the distant mountain peaks. He had last seen this holy man and woman on that evening long ago when he had said good-by at the Lehi depot. He remembered clearly the rounding nose and walrus mustache of his father, the thin lips and dark, worried eyes of his mother. Humorless, kind, and utterly scrupulous, they had lived in a state of salvation.

"I couldn't make it to the funeral of either of them," he said. "If it had been possible, I think I would have come. I was in New Jersey when Mother died, and I didn't get word of the funeral until three days after it was over. Dad died during the war, and I couldn't get a train in time. Everything was tied up in troop transportation."

Leah had momentarily moved to a nearby grave. "I can't stand these plastic flowers. They look shoddy so fast. I think I'll just take them in my purse and put them in the garbage can at the gate."

"I could have come to see them while they were alive, but I didn't."

"It's no use talking about things like that."

"I have come back to the church," Darrow said abruptly.

Leah's face was blank.

"I have been baptized again. I attend meetings. I pay tithing."

Across Leah's face, moving in quick succession, came surprise, fear of deception, and a curious mingling of rage and relief. "Why didn't you tell me?" she cried.

"Because it was tentative. It is still tentative."

Again incomprehension crossed her face.

"I have no word from God that I am forgiven."

"You don't need a word," Leah burst out indignantly. "If you obey, everything is all right." She embraced him, took his hand, pressed it to her cheek, looked into his face with tear-misted eyes. "Oh, Darrow, I am so happy, so very, very happy."

"I can't pay for what I have done to Father and Mother," he said.

"Oh, bother!" Leah said with vexation. "It doesn't matter at all. You are baptized again. They know it on the other side, Darrow, and they are so glad."

Darrow shook his head somberly. "They know what I have done with my life."

They walked on, arm in arm. Leah clung to Darrow like a sweetheart, tender, happy, doting. But even as she chatted about this cousin or that, he was seized by panic to see how age had come upon his sister. She was nothing like the image of the full-bloomed, heartyfleshed woman Darrow had carried in his mind for forty-five years. Her face was parched, her frame shrunken, her muscles reduced to taut wires. Nor could Darrow now put from his mind the bloody, premature death of Timothy Crofter or the terrible suffering of Karl Bjorlund, whose graves he had just seen. What had God intended when He created a world in which a face-eaten wretch was driven to bludgeon himself to death? The world was a book whose stories always ended in blood. Perhaps, as some said, the bloody endings were not God's meaning at all, but were the interpolation of mistranslating monks, dozing scribes, or old unvaliant Adam who relished the lustfruit of his curiosity. But perhaps the bloody endings were precisely God's meaning—an allegory of damnation written into the pages of the temporal world for all who had the sense to read.

Taking in the bright sun, the calls of birds in nearby trees, the reassuring hum of automobiles on the distant freeway, Darrow could almost persuade himself that the horrors and griefs of this graveyard had safely evaporated into the atmosphere. But not quite. He fancied he could hear a faint, persistent static from the graves about him—a muted, indistinguishable murmuring of subterranean voices. He imagined a sentience among the graves, a residual consciousness of the dead which had infiltrated the soil into which their bodies had corrupted: buried yearnings, passions ingrown with roots, pulsing aspirations locked in the clutch of the ground. He imagined that if he listened closely, if he strained to interpret, he could make out words piteous beyond all others. The dead were calling, "Here we are, Lord! See us! Save us!" Wasn't a cemetery a sign of hell? Its deathdread was symbolic and predictive of sinwrought man's horror of perdition.

At length Darrow and Leah came to a large plot enclosed by a picket fence of iron. A monumental shaft stood in the center of the plot. Its inscription read: *Joram Eastpark Sevy—Pioneer Founder—1824-1915.*

"Joram himself," Darrow said. "I remember the day he was buried."

"Here's Grandmother," Leah said as they entered the plot. They looked at the lettering on the polished black stone: *Seraphine Darrow—Fourth Wife of Joram Sevy—1848-1905.*

"She was gone before I was born," Darrow said.

"She changed my diapers many a time, Mother told me," Leah said. "Doesn't it make you feel good to see Grandfather's wives here with him? Of course, Martha Dean isn't here. Isn't that funny? Because she died on the plains before Grandfather had other wives, I almost forget he was ever married to her."

"And Ruhannah," Darrow said. "She isn't here, either."

"Well, of course not. What would you expect? She is buried in the cemetery on the avenues in Salt Lake City. She apostatized, you know. She was buried in an Episcopalian service.''

"Sara showed me Ruhannah's diary. I can't get out of my mind the possibility that Joram was guilty.''

"How can you say such a thing? You, of all people!'' Leah cried. "You were in his house dozens of times. Don't you remember how often Mother sent us to stay the night? We were supposed to keep an eye on Grandfather and Aunt Christine, but it was they who kept an eye on us.''

"What can you do with Ruhannah's diary?'' Darrow said. "Ruhannah seems to have been a sincere person.''

"Oh, yes, sincere! Sara likes to prate on about how genuine Ruhannah was and about how great her spiritual gifts were. Grandfather's other wives could have given you another side to that story. I had it over and over from Aunt Christine.''

"I wouldn't think Ruhannah would lie in her own diary.''

"She didn't lie; she exaggerated. Ruhannah turned every whisper of the Spirit into a shout. I'm not impressed by the spirituality of a woman who couldn't be decent to her sister wives. Ruhannah was all for herself. She never had a kind word for anybody else. She expected the other wives to worship her because she was singled out for special revelations and healings of the sick.''

Leah squatted and plucked a dandelion, then put it brusquely into her purse. Her voice was hoarse with disgust. "Sara says that Grandfather harried Ruhannah out of the church. That's silly. It isn't even a possibility. Ruhannah never had a testimony of the church. She had her own version of the Gospel, and she didn't know what it was to help build the kingdom. I don't know why she came to Zion in the first place. And Grandfather tolerated her. He never lifted a finger against her, not even when she was spreading that terrible story. His other wives scolded him for it; they said if he didn't defend himself his reputation would be ruined. He shrugged and said God would be his judge.''

"It's strange he wouldn't defend himself.''

"He didn't need to defend himself! Everybody knew what kind of man he was. Any traveler caught at night in Lehi stayed in Grandfather's house. He never charged a penny."

Darrow and Leah wandered among the stones of the plot. Coming to the fence, they paused. Leah fingered the blunt point of an iron picket. "Grandfather didn't shoot Johanssen, and Ruhannah knew it. Johanssen was killed accidentally. Shooting accidents occurred all the time in those days. They still occur all the time. But Ruhannah couldn't take polygamy. She never did accept Grandfather's other wives."

"It's bizarre that the old story hangs on," Darrow said.

"Don't doubt Grandfather," Leah said urgently. "You mustn't betray him. I couldn't stand it if you did."

Leah's fingers continued to play over the scrolls and pickets. She had begun to talk about the heroism with which Joram had endured the unbelievable rigors of pioneer life. She reminded Darrow that the teenaged Joram had been driven, with his parents and their other children, from a home in Missouri. Mobbers had seized their house, barn, and animals. A sister had died of dysentery during the trek to Illinois. In Nauvoo, Joram married Martha Dean and built a house of his own. He sold it for sixty dollars when the Saints were driven from Nauvoo in the winter of 1846. The next summer Joram joined the Mormon Battalion, leaving his wife and tiny daughter behind in the camp of the Saints. With his fellow soldiers Joram marched from Fort Leavenworth to San Diego—a walk of some two thousand miles. Discharged, he made his way to the Salt Lake Valley, arriving there only two months after the vanguard of Mormon pioneers had arrived on July 24, 1847. He learned that neither his wife nor his daughter had survived the terrible winter on the Iowa plains. A year later Joram married Ruhannah. Afterward he married other wives and made his headquarters in Lehi. By her own choice Ruhannah remained with her three children on the ranch in West Canyon. Five years before she denounced Joram and left the church she moved to Lehi, where she insisted that Joram build her a separate house. Joram became a pillar of the community; he served many terms as alderman and mayor of Lehi, and for many years he was a counselor in the Provo stake presidency.

"I know Grandfather would never kill a man," Leah said passionately. "I know because I knew him. I know because of the way I feel in my heart." She looked insistently into Darrow's eyes. "And you know it, too."

Darrow and Leah walked arm in arm, returning along the paths leading to the cemetery gate. A jet whined high overhead; a locust buzzed in a nearby tree. Darrow's world seemed suddenly washed in sunshine. He was cheered immensely by the affectionate little woman who clung to him. He perceived the return of a lapsed protection. Despite her shrunken, aged condition, he sensed that nothing essential had departed from her. He fancied that her dwindled body bloomed with grace, that it could not fail to revive, pulse, and flourish forever. Her fervent loyalty to Joram was contagious. Didn't a man like Joram merit confidence; didn't he deserve the benefit of the doubt? Darrow remembered a morning when he and Leah had slept in Joram's house. Aunt Christine, Joram's last surviving wife, had called that breakfast was ready. Darrow ran down the stairs to the kitchen. Behind him, pacing demurely, came Leah, her unstrapped shoes scraping along the hardwood floor of the hall. From outside, a metallic clinking sound had stopped; Joram, already at work in the toolshed, would have put down his mallet and punch. Set upon the oilcloth of the kitchen table were bowls of steaming oatmeal and plates of buttered toast and eggs fried sunnyside up. Joram clattered into the kitchen through an outside door, growling about the recalcitrance of a stricken leg. Grey hair bristled in a thick patch on his head and sprouted in coarse tufts from his eyebrows. He gripped Darrow's shoulder and patted Leah's head as he went by on his way to wash his hands at the sink. Remembering, Darrow recognized that Joram had not needed words; his mere presence was an utterance and a prophecy.

It was no accident that the family had made a hero of Joram, Darrow reflected. Without question he had been a man of extraordinary nerve and virtue. Under no circumstance could Joram have construed God's will as bent toward a bloody penance for sinful men; to think otherwise did dishonor both to him and to God. Hadn't God commanded men to love one another? Hadn't He told them, when offended, to turn the other cheek? Thinking well of Joram, Darrow could think better of himself. Surely there was something salvageable, something worthy of redemption, in Darrow Sevy.

A little after twelve, the general reunion of the Sevy family began with a lunch in a Lehi park. Darrow found a place in a line filing along serving tables loaded with cold cuts, casseroles, salads and breads of all sorts, fresh fruit, early corn, and countless pies and cakes. He sat to eat at a table where unfamiliar but amiable cousins made room for him. At two o'clock Darrow joined a crowd of his relatives in the recreation hall of a nearby church where the first session of the reunion convened. Near four o'clock, suffering from a headache, Darrow emerged from the church before the meeting had concluded.

On the steps a man sat whittling. "Hello, Darrow, how be?" he said. "It's me, Glen Sevy. You used to know me when I was just a big-assed kid." Glen wore stiff, unfaded Levi's, scuffed cowboy boots, and a pearl-buttoned shirt beneath which his stomach bulged. Beads of sweat stood on his tanned, bald head.

"Well, for sure, it's Glen, isn't it?" Darrow said.

"Yeah, it's me. I been meaning to speak to you all day. I had to get away from all the crap going on inside there. Can't take much in that line."

"It makes you want to be somewhere else, doesn't it?" Darrow agreed.

Glen laughed. "Kind of funny, though, the way they're clawing each other up in there. Old Uncle Samuel, he says, Now, your officers having duly met in Provo the other night, we endorse fully this fine manuscript of Cousin Claiborne's, which tells the whole truth and nothing but the truth about Grampa Sevy, and then that BYU professor, Morton Rickover, he leaps up and says, We ought to thank Cousin Claiborne for his great labors, he really has put together a wonderful book here, except it's all a bunch of lies about Ruhannah, and then Claiborne's boy Richard gets all heated up and he says, What do you mean this book don't tell the truth about Ruhannah and Grampa, and your good sister Leah goes running in swinging like a prizefighter and she says, How come we can't let these blackhearted falsehoods die and how long are we going to put up with this kind of libel against one of God's noble servants? God, I thought I'd die laughing." Glen stopped laughing abruptly. "I got to have a drink. Listen, I have a bottle in the car. Let's drive on down to a little bar I know on Geneva Road. They'll give us setups and we can recover from all that bullshit.''

"OK," Darrow said, "let's go talk awhile. But I'm strictly on soda pop.''

Several miles south of the Geneva steel mill they came to a bar named The Slagheap. Inside it was dim and cool. In a corner a woman with plump, half-exposed breasts played and sang at a piano.

"There's Dorothy," Glen said. "I was afraid we might be too early." He led Darrow to the piano. "Dorothy, honey, here's one of my cousins, Darrow Sevy. He's a good man from the East." The woman smiled at Darrow.

"How about 'By the Time I Get to Phoenix'?" Glen asked.

"Sure, after this one."

Glen led Darrow to a table. "Nice woman there. She'll play the old ones if you want her to. I'd sure like to get into her pants, but she don't take none of that. But she sure is nice."

They sat and Glen pulled a fifth of bourbon from a sack. "You won't change your mind, I guess?"

"No, thanks, just root beer for me," Darrow said.

"Mighty nice meal, that lunch today," Glen said. "Can't say I felt very comfortable, though. Don't none of them regard me anyhow. This liquor's the reason. I know that, and I know I got to get hold of it. Old Claiborne went by me in the hall just before the meeting and he says, Get off that goddamn liquor, Glen, though of course he didn't say goddamn. Then he just went on by. He don't size me up high as a dog turd."

"I know what you mean," Darrow said.

"Oh, hell," Glen said, laughing again, "wasn't that funny when old Uncle Knudson gets up during the introductions this afternoon? He's every inch of ninety-five. His voice quivers like an accordion and he says, I been around for a long time, I was thirty when Grampa died, I can't see and my arthritis is terrible, I ought to be in the cemetery but I ain't. Lord, that old goat! Samuel finally had to get up and cut him off so the meeting could go on."

At another table two women sipped beer and talked in low, confidential tones; with half-closed eyes one of them drew on her cigarette and exhaled a column of smoke. The smoky twilight of the bar depressed Darrow. It was too familiar; everything about the bar reminded him of his misspent years. He thought of the good mood he had been in after his visit to the cemetery with Leah. In this place he couldn't understand that mood at all.

He leaned forward. "Tell me, Glen, do you think Ruhannah was right? Did Joram kill Johanssen?"

"Why, hell yes, he done it. You think Sevys got a guarantee for sainthood?"

"I'm serious. Would he really do it?"

"Let me tell you something," Glen said. "Sevys ain't angels. You seen that boy Lester drifting around at lunch today? Lester Evans, Katie's boy? That boy is queer."

"He's what?"

"Gay. Fruitier than a Jell-O salad. He screws with men."

"Is that true?"

"Hell, yes. When you lift the cover off and look at what is underneath, there ain't anything you can't find in the Sevy family. Take that pious old fraud, Cousin Wilbur Jones. When my dad tried to get an option on Joram's sheep herds, Wilbur bribed the probate judge. He got the whole damn sheep business, all of it, everything Joram had built up in Cedar Valley and Rush Valley and even out in Skull Valley. Wilbur was chairman of the board—the one and only Rush Valley Land and Livestock Company. He's still on the board, but that stink-ass grandson of his is chairman—Benny. He ain't hardly thirty. I asked him, Benny, can I hunt deer up there on Joram's land in the Sheeprocks? And he says, Why sure, just line up and pay your twenty-dollar trespass fee like all the other hunters. Shit!"

Glen poured himself another drink. "Sure, Joram did it," he said. "You didn't know my dad much. You're supposed to love your dad, ain't you? Well, of all the dirty sons of bitches that ever lifted a hind leg and pissed on this earth, my dad was the dirtiest. I hate him and sometimes I wish he was still alive so I could show him how much. Do you know what he done to me? He took his belt off, lots of times, and he held me by the arm, and I circled around howling like a dog, and he whipped the living daylights out of me. I couldn't cough without him thinking I was sassing him.''

"Joram wouldn't do something like that," Darrow said. "I knew him.''

"You believe what you want. It don't make no difference to me. I sure as hell wouldn't get up in meeting and spout off the way Morton Rickover and that niece of yours does. But you take my dad again. Most of my life, I kept saying to myself, He was a good man, he didn't go to church and he smoked and all that, but he was my dad, and everybody knows your dad is the best guy there ever was. But I got to thinking about what he done one day when I was thirteen. I had a dog, Cockleburr, part collie. God, I loved him; he was the only thing that held me together. One day Dad says, Call that dog in so we can get back to town. The dog wouldn't come in a hurry; he was fooling around a dead sheep across the creek. Dad took out the thirty-thirty and shot him in front of my eyes. It took me until I was forty to figure out what Dad really wanted. It wasn't the dog he wanted to kill. It was me.''

"It doesn't fit with Joram.''

"Sure it fits. I treated my kids the same way. I kicked the shit out of them about once a week just to keep them tuned up good. I got it from my dad. And where did my dad get to wanting blood? He got it from his dad, and his dad got it from Joram. Don't be fooled by how pious Joram got in his old age. After them Missouri pukes and Illinois mobbers pushed the Mormons around so long, why hell, our boys was just as mean and ugly as the pukes and mobbers ever was.''

"It isn't possible that Joram wanted blood," Darrow protested. "If he had shot Johanssen, he wouldn't have done it in anger. He would have thought he was doing Johanssen a favor.''

"People don't never kill nobody unless they're mad. Maybe they don't think they're mad, but they are.''

"No, you're wrong," Darrow insisted. "He would have thought of it as a sacred ritual. He wouldn't have been angry.''

Glen turned his glass in his fingers. He stared at its gyration with befuddled eyes. "So I might be wrong—could be, easy enough.'' Then he brightened. "Maybe God is the one who started it—

wanting blood, I mean. Suppose that son of a bitch Johanssen had it coming. Suppose he needed to be cleaned up."

"It couldn't be true."

"I ain't never noticed God being put off by a little blood," Glen said. "Everybody says He put His own son up for crucifixion, don't they? God's up there keeping an eye on the earth and He says, All you people down there swilling around cheating and drinking and carrying on, can't you act decent for one little minute? Well, I'll fix that; I'll damn your hides to hell."

"That's a terrible thing to believe."

"I'm just bullshitting. I don't know nothing about anything." Glen scratched his shoulder and poured another drink. "But I ain't going to back down on what I said about Joram. He done it, no doubt about it. In 1954 or somewhere around there, Bentley and me drove up West Canyon to the old place. There wasn't much left, but the foundation of Ruhannah's house was there. The chimney was still standing. It was chiseled rock; I don't know who chiseled it. Out back a ways there was some poles where the old corral used to be. Bentley says, Glen, he shot him by the corral. I says, Who told you so? Bentley says, Dad told me. Johanssen asked Joram to tie him to the poles so he wouldn't fall in the dirt, and then Joram went back and leaned against a juniper so he could shoot steady, and then he shot him in the heart. So maybe it was a ritual. But you don't kill nobody unless you want their blood."

"How could he do it?" Darrow said. "That fall I turned seventeen there was a terrible accident in Pole Canyon. I was hunting deer with Father and Uncle Todd and three of Uncle Todd's boys. This old fellow—a guy from Goshen or one of those little towns at the end of the lake—this old fellow got the early blurs and he shot his own grandson. He shot at him two or three times before he hit him, and then he hit him in the ear. There wasn't anything left on that side of his head. Father helped carry the kid's body, and I came along to carry the guns. The kid's jaw was loose, just hanging by some sinews, and every so often it would catch on a branch and flop down and dangle, and the old man would shove it back into place, and he kept saying, I thought it was a deer."

"God Almighty," Glen said, "I wouldn't never be able to hunt deer again."

"So I guess I don't believe the story about Joram," Darrow said. "How could he go through his life remembering something like that? What would he think when he cut Johanssen off the poles? What would he say to Ruhannah? He couldn't just go back to the house and say, Ruhannah, wash that man's body up nice and clean for burial. Don't pay any attention to what the bullet did to his chest, and I'll just fix up a nice coffin and—"

"There wasn't no coffin."

"How do you know there wasn't? They wouldn't bury him without a coffin!"

"We dug him up."

"You dug him up!"

"Yeah. I'm kind of ashamed of it, but we done it. Bentley says, Glen, why don't we see if he's still there? There was this pile of rocks on the other side of the corral, just like Bentley had always heard. We cleaned off the rocks and dug down, and by damn, we found some bones. We put them back later. Looked like a couple of leg bones, a vertebra or two, and some others I couldn't make out. There wasn't no coffin."

"Why wouldn't they have a coffin?"

"They used wagon tarp in them days. They didn't have nothing else."

Glen drove Darrow to Leah's house and the two cousins said good-by. In the evening Darrow and Leah went to the social assembly of the reunion. Sara waved to them from the opposite side of the crowded recreation hall. The program, a welter of amateur presentations and impromptu expressions, was a comforting distraction to Darrow. He took refuge in the murmurs of approval which flowed through the audience as representatives of family branches recited poems, sang songs, bore testimonies, and recounted family lore. For a while he slipped from his fretful individuality into the soothing mass of the family. He roused with instinctive alarm to the strident voice of a cousin, Ruth Boker, who walked onto the stage to announce a skit on the life of Joram. She needed volunteers from the audience to fill out the cast of a *tableau*

vivant accompanying a narrative poem she had composed. Darrow
sank as deep as he could into his chair, but Ruth came from the stage
expressly to get him. Leah enthusiastically pushed him toward
Ruth's outstretched hand.

In a moment the figures were established on the stage. In the
center a man and woman and six children represented the family of
Joram's father and mother during the Missouri and Illinois persecutions. On one side of the stage a young man wearing a military
bandolier and holding a musket represented Joram during his service in the Mormon Battalion. On the other side, wearing an oldtime
coat and holding Scriptures in his hand, stood Darrow, representing
Joram when he was a leader in the stake and community. A piano
accompanist let her fingers race into a flourishing introduction.
Ruth, overweight, perspiring, indomitably cheerful, began the
recitation of a lengthy poem with a frequent refrain:

> A great-grandfather wise, to the Gospel true,
> He was ever attentive the Lord's will to do.
> He suffered mobbers, deserts, Lamanites too,
> He triumphed over all for me and you.

Darrow broiled in the blinding stage lights. Someone had turned
off the air-conditioning of the hall and had opened a row of double
outside doors. During lulls in the recitation Darrow heard the chir-
rup of crickets and the passing of cars on the street outside. He
sensed that Ruth had honored him by assigning him the most impos-
ing station in the tableau of Joram's life; undoubtedly the word of
his rebaptism was getting around. But Darrow withered. He was a
fraud, an imposter; he could not play Joram. Beyond the stage
lights was the ominous power of his assembled uncles and aunts and
cousins. Glen had been wrong to emphasize the corruptions of the
Sevys; whatever their individual failings might be, together they
evoked a monumental righteousness. The collective weight of their
decent eyes was a burden Darrow could scarcely support.

The image of Glen's sweaty, suntanned faced appeared and reappeared in his mind, drifting like the clouds of cigarette smoke in
the dismal light of The Slagheap. The rage and passion of Glen's
words dinned in his ears. Darrow strained to remember the elusive

truth Glen had uttered: *Suppose that son of a bitch Johanssen had it coming. Suppose he needed to be cleaned up.* All at once Darrow was staggered by an illumination. He had grasped what no one else had understood. In its season, bloody sacrifice was just. Ruhannah was right: Joram had killed Johanssen. But he had killed him in righteousness and was no less heaven's hero.

Darrow looked askance at Ruth, whose interminable poem went on. His anger surged. Ruth's recitation seemed innocent enough, a pulpy trifle, a mere nuisance like the jangling of a telephone when one wishes to concentrate. Yet her poem was a parody of Joram's life. It was another episode in the perennial pageant of a deodorized, mythical Joram. *There are sins for which men, if they had their eyes open to their true condition, would be perfectly willing to have their own blood spilt upon the ground, that the smoke thereof might ascend to heaven as an offering for their sins.* Why had the Saints resisted Brigham Young's counsel? Why had Brigham himself gone back on it? These assembled Sevys were shunners and weakhearts. They were loath to admit that men and women passed to heaven only in horror and blood. They preferred to believe that the dying pierced the veil without throes, as if human beings were made of paper and could be neatly folded, inserted into envelopes, metered, bagged, and mailed intact into eternity.

Darrow exulted. His spirits rose, and a courage he had never felt before came over him. He saw the certainty of his salvation. With an absolute sympathy he intuited the guilty heart of Johanssen, for whom the roar of Joram's rifle had been the most tender of mercies. With a burst of emotion he understood the beauty of flagellation. He yearned for the strokes of the whip, for the lovely cleansing of pain. He had been hostage to the prince of darkness and had not known how to ransom himself. But there was a way. He had authority from Joram. Darrow's blood was his wergild. This very body, this rich hoard of pain, was his shriveprice, a sufficient collateral to buy off wrath, to unbond him from damnation. There was but a single technicality: his self-destruction must be a rite, a ceremony. It would have to proceed with propriety and order.

The Christianizing of Coburn Heights

God had blessed Coburn Heights, a suburb on the east bench of Salt Lake City where wealthy Saints shared with their Gentile neighbors the pleasures of wide, curving streets, spacious houses, and driveways cluttered with motor homes, power boats, and snowmobiles. The foremost shepherd of the faithful in this prosperous suburb was Sherman Colligan, president of Coburn Heights stake. On a wintry Saturday morning Sherman shopped for his wife in Albertson's supermarket, pushing a shopping cart containing a growing mound of beef roast, pickles, muffins, potato chips, Postum, and all kinds of things which make life tolerable. A few feet into the pet food aisle he stopped abruptly. Coming toward him was a tattered, crooked little woman who might have emerged from the cargo bin of a garbage truck. She wore a soiled brown dress, askew at the hem and pinned at the breast. Dark cotton stockings sagged on her bony legs; warped, scuffed shoes slopped on her feet. Staring at her, Sherman realized that she was lopsided because her entire left side was atrophied: her leg was shortened, her arm dwindled, her breast shrunken, her cheek and ear diminished. She listed and leaned, having not two sides, but one and a half.

The woman pulled a yellow wagon in which she had set her wadded coat, four sixpacks of orange soda pop, and a box of macaroni and cheese. Intuitively Sherman knew her. She had to be Rendella Kranpitz, the bizarre newcomer whose bishop had threatened to excommunicate her for contentiousness. Sherman had found the charge incredible; no one was excommunicated these days for contentiousness. The little woman came up against Sherman's shopping cart and stopped. He blinked, looking closer to see whether this woman truly had, as her bishop claimed, a heart for fire and rage, a will for running against the wind, for rupturing barricades, for trampling down the walls of the world.

The woman looked Sherman up and down, then put forth her strong right arm and shook his hand. "You're President Colligan," she said. "If I were you, I wouldn't let that second counselor—what's his name—conduct at stake conference anymore. He isn't up to snuff. No way at all."

"It's certainly nice to meet a new member of my stake," Sherman said pleasantly.

The woman continued to shake his hand. "I would sure spruce up my stake conferences if I were you. When that choir sang last time, you could have laid me out square for being on a goat farm."

"You must be Sister Kranpitz," Sherman said warmly.

She dropped his hand and eyed him suspiciously. "How come you know my name?"

"Bishop Bosen has told me about you."

"So what's he say about me behind my back? That's what I'd like to know!"

"Nothing but the best. He says you're a good, faithful sister." Sherman, whose large frame carried fifty pounds of excess weight, towered over the little woman. He wore galoshes and a checkered overcoat and a narrow-brimmed hat. He tried to amplify the friendly smile which he made it a policy to carry on his round, clean-shaven face.

"Say," Rendella said, "do you have all the Articles of Faith memorized?"

"Not entirely," Sherman said. "I once had."

Rendella fixed her eyes on a shelf of bags filled with dried dog food and began to recite. "First: We believe in God, the Eternal Father, and in his Son Jesus Christ, and in the Holy Ghost. Second: We believe that men will be punished for their own sins, and not for Adam's transgressions. Third: We believe—"

"That's excellent," Sherman interrupted with an admiring exhalation of breath. "It looks like you have every one of them down pat."

Rendella wandered to the side of Sherman's shopping cart. She picked up a bottle of expensive grape juice, shook it, and peered suspiciously at the label. "That isn't wine," Sherman said. "It's grape juice imported from Germany."

Rendella put the bottle down and picked up a jar of peanut butter. "That peanut butter isn't any good," she said. "There aren't any bits in it." She tried without success to unscrew the lid and then returned the jar to the cart.

"Who's your dad?" she said. "He isn't one of those Colligans from Kanab, is he?"

"Our line never got farther south than Provo. Actually my dad was—"

"That's good," Rendella interrupted. "Those Kanab Colligans aren't worth a bucket of peach pits. Really, you know, you've got to do something about this stake. I never saw a worse one in my life. Some of the sermons that get preached in the fifth ward would puke a turkey."

"I don't know about that. It seems to me we've got a pretty good stake. In fact, it's one of the best in the entire church."

"I can preach, but nobody ever asks me to," Rendella said. "Maybe you don't think I can preach," she added bitterly.

"I don't doubt you can preach. Why not? The gift of eloquence is given to many."

"People think I'm crazy, but I'm not."

"Why would anybody think that?" Sherman said congenially. "You're just another good, faithful servant of the Lord."

She looked down at her dress. "What do you expect when somebody has to wear rags like these?"

Sherman brightened. "We can fix that in a minute. Bishop Bosen will get you a welfare order and we'll get you some nice dresses."

She stiffened. "Are you trying to tell me I don't dress so good?"

"Golly, no," Sherman said.

"Who did you say your dad was? My dad was Simon B. Kranpitz.

He lived in Monroe for seventy-eight years, and he was never anything but a ward clerk. And then they went and made Ranny Jackson second counselor when Chad Hislop got made bishop, and Dad said, That's it—when old Ranny Jackson gets made counselor and they pass me by, I quit. And he never went to church again."

"I'm sorry to hear that."

Rendella put her hand into her pocket and pulled out a candy bar. She looked at it a moment, glanced up at Sherman, and thrust it back into her pocket. "You think I'm not going to pay for that, don't you?" she said angrily. She pulled the bar out and placed it on a sixpack of orange soda pop in her wagon. "Don't ever say I steal anything!"

She smoothed the front of her dress. "Who did you say your folks were? What kind of uppities were they?"

"My folks were just ordinary people."

"How come you got this job then?" she said. "Let's see what you know. Tell me what this Scripture means." She drew herself up on her longer leg and said in an oratorical tone: "Lamentations, chapter four, verse twenty-one: Rejoice and be glad, O daughter of Edom, that dwellest in the land of Uz; the cup also shall pass through unto thee: thou shalt be drunken, and shalt make thyself naked."

Sherman hemmed and looked about uncomfortably.

"So what does it mean?" she insisted. "You're supposed to be the stake president and you don't know anything."

A half-hour later Sherman sat in his car in the Albertson's parking lot, eating a doughnut. He had been wise enough to order thirteen doughnuts at the bakery stand; finding an even dozen, his wife would have no reason to be disappointed with him for breaking his diet. Grey winter clouds lowered over Coburn Heights; the parking lot was icy with the remnants of last week's storm. As Sherman pulled out his handkerchief to wipe away the final crumbs, he saw Rendella Kranpitz emerge from the grocery store. The sleeves of her black coat draped over her hands and the hem hung nearly to her ankles. Pulling her wagon, she lurched erratically across the parking lot. Heedless of speeding cars, she jaywalked across the nearby boulevard and disappeared into a side street. Sherman looked at his watch and decided that he had time to visit Arthur Bosen, bishop of the ward in which Rendella lived.

Arthur was in his backyard dredging out his goldfish pond for the winter. At Sherman's insistence, Arthur went on with his work as they talked. Chunks of ice lay about the perimeter of the pool, from which Arthur scooped bucketsful of water. Sherman admired the look of outdoor competence which Arthur's woolen cap and quilted ski jacket gave him. Arthur Bosen was the best of Sherman's seven bishops. He was punctual in making his reports and successful in turning out his quotas of members for temple work and welfare assignments. Sherman and Arthur had been good friends since high school days and in private had dispensed with the formality of calling one another President Colligan and Bishop Bosen.

"I just met Rendella Kranpitz at Albertson's," Sherman said.

Arthur scrutinized Sherman closely. "You seem to have come out of the experience unscathed."

"Are you still thinking about excommunicating her?"

"You better believe it!" Arthur muttered grimly as he dredged up a shovelful of muck and dumped it into a standing wheelbarrow.

"Is the problem all that bad?"

"It's worse," Arthur declared. Three months of that woman were too much for any ward. Rendella Kranpitz was retarded or insane, or, more likely, both. She had come from a small town in Sevier County; Arthur couldn't for the moment remember which one. By an appalling fluke of circumstances she had inherited a house in Coburn Heights. The trustee of her inherited estate was a Gentile lawyer whose office was in downtown Salt Lake. He was a civil liberties crank who resented the way society treated children, prisoners, and idiots, and he protected Rendella in the possession of her house. Rendella had a spirit of deceit and disruption. In any church meeting where there was the slightest possibility that she could take the floor and speak, she usurped time and corrupted purposes. In the monthly testimony meeting she invariably rose and, instead of briefly bearing her testimony, entered upon a lengthy sermon, peeling off in her arrogant voice incessant strings of Scriptural passages and quotations from modern prophets and apostles. She exhorted, chided, and berated, and when at last she became silent and sat down, she had brought her fellow worshipers to a seething boil.

"She belongs in an asylum," Arthur concluded vindictively.

"You are exaggerating, of course," Sherman said, chuckling with appreciation for Arthur's ironies.

"You can't exaggerate anything in the case of this woman."

"Well," said Sherman, "we are after all the guardians of the unfortunate."

"I thought maybe I was the unfortunate one."

"Sometimes the Lord gives us a burden that is a blessing in disguise."

"This one is burden all the way through."

"We owe special care to those who can't make distinctions between good and evil."

"She isn't one of that kind. She knows exactly how to go for the jugular every time."

It appeared that Arthur's ironies were not ironies; he really meant to excommunicate Rendella Kranpitz. A pity for this little woman had come over Sherman. Wasn't she, after all, a spirit child of their Father in Heaven? Wasn't she a spirit sister to Sherman himself? And to Arthur? The warrior in Sherman Colligan began to awake. He heard martial trumpets, the hoofbeats of warhorses, the clash and clatter of swords. He was proud of his stake; his people tithed with unusual generosity, and they achieved outstanding percentages in home teaching and church attendance. Sherman himself was a model for the members of his stake. He had risen to a vice-presidency in a savings and loan company in the city. He took courses in motivation and management. He had a lust for challenge, resistance, and obstacles. His thick chest and broad shoulders suggested solidity, drive, the ability to move and to make move. Yet his fine face beamed with kindness and good sense. The man of arms within him was tamed to Christian purposes; he was tuned entirely to the pastoral services of his calling. He forgave the sinful, comforted the bereaved, sustained the wavering. He prayed for himself and his people a proper testing, a sufficient trial to keep them alert, spiritually fecund, resistant to the softening which comes with abundance and blessings.

"We can't abandon this poor sister," Sherman said. His voice vibrated with compassion. "Excommunicate her! We think a missionary does well to *convert* one person during a two-year mission. Isn't it worth as much to *save* one who is already with us—the one lost sheep strayed from the ninety-nine that are found?"

Arthur leaned disconsolately on his shovel. "It was the other ninety-nine I had in mind when I thought about excommunicating her."

Sherman waved his hand impatiently. "Gosh, man, we owe the Heavenly Father some service for all these blessings he has given us. Look at us here, you and me, standing in this two-acre oakbrush lot of yours. This land alone, without your house and improvements, has got to be worth thirty thousand."

"If we have many like Rendella Kranpitz around, it won't be worth two hundred."

"She balances you out, don't you see? She puts you on your mettle. Just think of her as a test. You'll be surprised how quick you get on top of all these problems." Sherman could see that Arthur was wavering; he had never been a match for Sherman in an argument. Sherman slapped him on the back. "Cheer up, brother! This woman was put in your ward for a special reason. Who else could handle her the way you can?"

"Dang it, Sherm, I just don't have the spirit to wrestle with her anymore. You don't know what she's like."

"Of course I know what she's like. I just saw her in the grocery store, didn't I? Are you going to admit you can't outthink that poor disadvantaged creature? Just put yourself into her frame of mind and think ahead of her; anticipate her. You'll come up with some solutions."

Arthur shook his head dolefully. "So far it's been her who outthinks me. Every time."

Sherman put his arm around Arthur; the old technique of loving a subordinate into compliance always worked. "Come on now, Art. No more of that excommunication talk. OK?"

"Well, sure," Arthur said, "if that's what you want, we'll give her another go."

"That's the talk I like to hear! That's what I like about you, Art, and always have. You're Christian all the way through, and you've got drive and guts and energy. Go do'er, man! Keep up your courage, say your prayers, and tear into it. You can't fail!''

Later, thinking about the little matter involving Arthur and Rendella Kranpitz, Sherman had the warm feeling of a duty well done. He didn't doubt for a moment that Arthur would come up with a total solution; Arthur had always underrated his own capacities. As for Rendella, Sherman was happy to have done some small thing in behalf of another of the souls entrusted to his care. That's what made management and leadership rewarding, whether in Sherman's professional life or in the work of the church. He always felt that what he did was vital; it touched lives and helped people.

On a Sunday evening two weeks later, as Sherman sat by the fire working on a church report, his wife escorted into the living room a sober-looking delegation. It was a high-powered group from the fifth ward, heavy with rank and distinction even by the standards of Coburn Heights. The three men were a physician, an insurance executive, and the owner of a supermarket; the two women were a state legislator and a hospital trustee. Uttering a hearty welcome, Sherman had an uneasy intuition that he must distract his visitors. He pointed out a painting hanging on the wall; it was a primitive work of Nauvoo, done by one of Sherman's forebears—a priceless heirloom. Harmon Roylance, the physician and the apparent spokesman of the group, scarcely noticed. It was unusual, Brother Roylance admitted in a grim, braced voice, for church members to rise spontaneously like a posse of vigilantes, but they had been driven to it by the excesses of Rendella Kranpitz.

"I believe Bishop Bosen is taking care of that problem," Sherman said.

"Yes," Brother Roylance agreed, "like a man fighting a lion with a toothpick. And he says you say there's nothing to be done about it."

There were items of behavior which the bishop might not have made known to President Colligan, the physician said. Rendella Kranpitz was always abroad. On certain days of the week she ranged beyond the boundaries of the fifth ward. People humored her in her claim to be an agent for Deseret Industries; she often dragged her yellow wagon home loaded with old furniture or clothes, which she stockpiled in her house on the pretense of calling in a thrift-store truck. But no truck had ever come, and the interior of her house was sordid with debris. Her yard was kept decent only by the unsolicited efforts of neighbors whom Rendella was more likely to berate for trespassing than to thank for their services. On other days Rendella worked within the fifth ward, where she exploited certain timid, selfless sisters. She rang doorbells and asked to come in for visits. Some sisters bluntly refused; others cowered silently behind their drawn drapes while Rendella repeatedly rang their doorbells. But a few responded and let her in. Once there, she stayed all day and ate lunch and sometimes supper, following the housewife around her home with incessant tales of scandalous behavior among ward members and church authorities.

During the week just past she had delivered a political tract from door to door throughout much of Coburn Heights. Brother Roylance put a copy of the tract on the coffee table before Sherman. On it was the photograph of a frantic-looking man with a receding chin and bulging eyes. The pamphlet announced the candidacy of Alphonse D. Farthingage for president of the United States in an election still a year and half away. Mr. Farthingage proposed a simple platform: if elected, he promised to open negotiations with the occupants of the numerous UFO's intruding in earth's airspace, in hopes of welding them into a coalition against the Soviet Union. The text of the pamphlet went on to imply that the general authorities of the church supported Mr. Farthingage.

"Can you imagine how much this woman is doing singlehandedly to damage the image of the church in Coburn Heights?" Brother Roylance said in a voice which had become increasingly melancholy.

That led him to the most insufferable of her traits—worse than her bizarre body, her unkempt clothes, her predatory raids upon the neighborhood, her obscene house, her constant disruption of church services. It was her arrogance, her desire to insult, her aggressive will to attack, accuse, and provoke.

"There's only one thing to do," Brother Roylance said, chopping the air with an emphatic hand. "Cut her off! Get her out of the

church. Even if we can't put her out of the neighborhood, we don't
have to associate her with the name of the church."

The other members of the delegation broke into a medley of accusation and protest.

"We're ashamed to be Mormons!"

"She's undercutting the missionary work."

"My kids don't learn disrespect in the streets. They learn it in
church."

"We paid for that chapel. I shelled out twenty-five hundred
dollars! You'd think I'd get to enjoy it. Either she goes or I go."

The accumulation of angry respectability cowed Sherman; he
shook and quivered with the blows. Then his stubbornness re-
surged, his anger flared up. He resented these unvaliant brothers
and sisters; even more, he resented that lurching, off-centered, cun-
ning fraction of a woman who could singlehandedly obstruct the
function of one of the most successful stakes in the church. He
became determined. Whether she liked it or not, whether they liked
it or not, this woman would go forward in the sustaining fellowship
and sanctifying ordinances of the fifth ward of the Coburn Heights
stake.

Sherman took the offensive. "So," he fulminated, "you can't
cope. A ward filled with fifty-thousand-dollar-a-year people—
college graduates, professionals, members of Rotary, Kiwanis, and
the Exchange—and you can't cope. God Almighty didn't set up
wards and stakes to save 99 percent of the members; he set them up
to save 100 percent. Are you telling me we aren't a 100 percent
stake?"

Sherman glared about scornfully. The members of the delegation
appeared crestfallen, confused, ready to search their memories to
see what they had failed to understand.

Sherman stood and walked up and down before the delegation.
He turned to one of the sisters, thrust out his arm, and fingered the
sleeve of his shirt. "That's a forty-dollar shirt—a luxury. Shall I
take God's fine gifts without any pity for someone who doesn't have
so much as a normal body?"

He turned to the fireplace and put another log in the fire. "Well,
go ahead if you've just got to," he said wearily. "Throw her to the

Gentiles. We won't try to save anybody in Coburn Heights who isn't rich and beautiful to start with.''

Tears welled in the eyes of one woman. The men fidgeted and stared at the floor. In one of those moments of inspiration which sometimes came to Sherman in the heat of tough action, he saw what must be done—a plan, a coordinated program to rehabilitate Rendella Kranpitz. He became intense. His voice varied in pitch, it rang with vision and purpose. "We're going forward. I promise action. I will personally assist Bishop Bosen to devise a plan that will solve this problem. We will energize the entire fifth ward. We will not cast off this woman.''

Sherman sat again, took up his pen, and, while he talked, doodled on a pad of paper. Formless, incoherent lines, loops, scratches fell into order. Two words appeared: *firmness, love.* Magic ideas, unfailing principles. In the matter of firmness, the authorities would insist that Rendella conform. No more invasions of private homes, no more slovenliness, no more lengthy, out-of-place speeches. She had to know where the limits were, and she had to respect them, order being a divine commandment, an eternal fact to which the human spirit had to adapt itself. In the matter of love—well, wasn't this a great opportunity, an exciting chance to show how the Gospel really worked? Sherman's face glowed; he gestured with open hands. The entire ward must join together in an outpouring of love which would inundate Rendella with reassurance and sweep away her fractiousness like so much debris in a roaring river.

Sherman sensed that he was clear at last. The good people of the delegation were behind him now. The eyes of the women lighted with admiration and the men nodded their assent. Still, he had the feeling that he had won by only a millimeter, and after the group had gone he dialed Arthur.

"I just lost a patch of skin, Art,'' he said unhappily. "That was low of you to turn that delegation loose on me.''

"I didn't undercut you,'' the bishop said after Sherman had told him about the visit. "Those people are smart enough to figure things out for themselves.''

"Whip them into line, can't you?''

"Whip them into line! It's that woman who is out of line.''

"I hope you're remembering what I told you about outthinking her."

"Heck, I can't catch up with her long enough to outthink her. She's got the ball all the time."

"Look, I've got a solution for you. It came to me when that bunch was here a few minutes ago. You'll get the whole fifth ward into this. You'll redo that woman; you'll rehabilitate her; you'll give her a new personality."

Arthur groaned into the telephone. "I'm burned out, Sherm. Why don't you do it?"

"A violation of administrative principle. This is a ward problem. You and your counselors have got to deal with it."

"No way, Sherm."

"What do you mean, no way?"

"I mean I didn't want this bishop's job in the first place. I got nothing against you, Sherm; you're the best. But I resign, right now."

"Look, Art, I didn't mean you had to do it alone. I'll help you with this Rendella Kranpitz thing. OK?"

"I don't know," Arthur said. "It really felt good to say I resign."

"This isn't any time for joking. The first step is for you and me to call on Sister Kranpitz."

A mood of near invincibility had come over Sherman. He was convinced that all would go well, that the disturbance of mind and spirit which afflicted Rendella Kranpitz would be reversed by a bold application of Gospel principles. Nonetheless, when Sherman and Arthur called on Rendella on a Tuesday evening, Sherman brought along Celia, his wife, as an added precaution. Rendella's yard, which lay under a mantle of snow, was not so unusual for Coburn Heights, but the interior of the house jolted Sherman. In the living room relics of fine furniture groaned beneath bundles of newspapers and cardboard boxes from which cast-off clothing dangled. A disorganized mountain of shoeboxes covered one wall. Some were shut tight; others had spilled out ball bearings, yarn remnants, and aquarium gravel. A broken rocking chair sat upside down in a corner. On the coffee table, as if serving as a centerpiece, was a large broiling pan filled nearly to the brim with rancid cooking grease.

Firmness and love: these were the principles Sherman repeated to himself as he set a small, broken drill press onto the floor and sat down in the chair it had occupied. Disciplining himself to a total candor, Sherman told Rendella that her behavior was unacceptable for a member of the fifth ward of the Coburn Heights stake. He forced himself to speak slowly and emphatically as he explained the offenses she had committed. Then he went on to cheer and entice her by explaining that, using welfare funds, they intended to buy appealing new clothes for her and to arrange for a visit to a hair salon. Several fine sisters of the ward were to be called to help her in grooming and dress. Families would invite her to supper several times a week. Certain couples would call for her on Sunday and take her to meetings—making sure, of course, that she was well dressed and groomed.

Braced by her strong leg, Rendella crowded into the corner of an armchair. Her eyes roamed everywhere in the room. Sherman was disconcerted by the relentless, cross-grained squint of her mouth and the startling disparity of her left side, upon which the limbs and features of a smaller person seemed to have been grafted. She was dressed in a faded green bakery uniform; a rip along the thigh was closed by six brass safety pins. She did not seem at all impressed by what he was saying. She could not help hearing, yet when he was through he saw that she had not heard.

"How come nobody ever asks me to be a Sunday School teacher?" she said peevishly.

"We don't aspire to particular callings in the church," Sherman said. "We do whatever we are asked to do."

"Well, I want to know what my calling is. How come I don't have a calling?"

"Your calling?" Sherman paused a moment, then saw an opening. "Yes, well, your calling is what I've just been telling you about. Your calling is to reform your life a little." Sherman congratulated himself on his ability to seize the moment. He patiently explained again what had been unacceptable about Rendella's behavior and what excellent new things awaited her.

"What kind of bishop do you call him?" she interrupted, pointing at Arthur. "You think he's a good bishop! Word going around is he's playing hankypanky with more than one. I could tell you who with, if you wanted to know."

"What next?" Arthur moaned, rolling his eyes in frustration.

"I absolutely will not tolerate that kind of talk," Sherman roared. "I know for a fact that Bishop Bosen is a righteous man." Rendella shrank. "Well, I just wanted to know what my calling is. How come nobody ever asks me to pray? Sister Jenson has got asked to pray five times in the past three months."

"Gosh," Arthur said, "I don't keep track of how many times people get asked to pray."

"He won't let me sing in the ward choir," Rendella said to Sherman. "I got all practiced up and now I don't get to sing."

"It was Sister Hanney's decision."

"You backed her up!"

Arthur turned toward Sherman. "Sister Hanney likes the choir to sing a cappella. She let Sister Kranpitz practice with the choir for three weeks; she even let her sing with them in Sacrament Meeting once." Arthur paused and shook his head in disbelief. "A whole choir off key—thirty of them! Sister Hanney stopped them twice to get back on pitch, but it didn't help."

"Sister Hanney is a third cousin to that Tinford bunch in Salina. That's why she doesn't like me. Ever since Grandfather Kranpitz beat old man Tinford for alderman in Richfield, those Tinfords have been down on the Kranpitzes."

"Maybe it would help if you didn't sing so loud," Arthur said.

"See!" Rendella said to Sherman. "Right there is what is wrong with the music in this ward. They're all afraid of somebody who can sing louder than they can."

The bishop shrugged and slumped into his chair.

Sherman cleared his throat and began again. He gestured emphatically to fix her attention as he explained once more the changes to which she would have to submit. Rendella's eyes wandered. In a moment they came to rest on Celia.

"Why doesn't she say something?" Rendella said. "You're looking peaked, honey." Rendella got up, hobbled into the kitchen, and returned with a bottle and a tablespoon. She poured out a spoonful of dark, gummy liquid and offered it to Celia. "Take this. It'll build your blood."

"Gracious, no, thanks; I just couldn't," Celia protested in a fluttery voice, whereupon Rendella spooned the liquid into her own mouth, gave the spoon an additional lick, and set it and the bottle on the coffee table.

At that moment, just as his will was beginning to waver, Sherman was struck by a brilliant idea. He sized it up and recognized it as inspiration. He called Arthur to a whispered conference in the hallway.

"Let's call her to be a Sunday School teacher."

Arthur's eyes bulged incredulously.

"We'll schedule her in one of your classrooms, and we'll call four couples to attend her class for three months. Then we'll rotate."

Arthur still had the appearance of a strangled man.

"It'll work. It'll be the outlet she needs. And it's the bargaining point we need. The people can put up with her because it's a call and won't last forever."

Sherman led Arthur into the living room. "Sister Kranpitz," he said, "we have decided to call you to be a Sunday School teacher in the fifth ward."

Rendella's face froze. Then her eyes shifted suspiciously from Sherman to Arthur, and again to Sherman. She asked what kind of class it would be. Sherman looked expectantly at Arthur, who had not recovered his speech. Well, that didn't matter, Rendella said, if it was a real Sunday School class. Did he mean a real Sunday School class? Arthur finally spoke, though weakly; it would be a Gospel Doctrine class—a special course for adults. Rendella relaxed in her chair and beamed with pleasure. She wanted to know if they could go over to the bishop's office right now and get a manual. Arthur said he would drop one by after work the next evening.

Rendella limped into her bedroom and returned with a copy of the Bible. "Some people say I don't know the Gospel," she said defiantly. She patted the book and tapped her own forehead with a finger. "I know it, all right. You'll see I can teach."

Then Sherman drove his bargains. The class was conditional

upon Rendella's accepting the changes he had been talking about. He knew now that she listened, and point by point he coerced her assent. She must allow some of the sisters to help her dress more nicely; she must call in the truck from Deseret Industries and clear her house of trash; she must stop scouring the neighborhood with her wagon; she must not give lengthy discourses in testimony meeting. In return, she would have nice clothes, invitations to supper, friends to take her to meeting. And, of course, her Sunday School class.

The plan was in effect by the following Sunday—another testimony to the efficiency of Sherman Colligan. He followed up every call Arthur made. He stayed on the telephone for hours, assuring the brothers and sisters who had been asked to assume duties in behalf of Sister Kranpitz that their assignment had come from the Lord. The plan, if carried out with enthusiasm and energy, could not fail.

On Sunday night reports of a startling success came in. Brother Horrup, who had been called to attend Rendella's class, telephoned Sherman to express his satisfaction. He and his wife were proud that their little bit had helped. He had a revised opinion of Rendella. Her lesson had followed the manual closely. He was especially impressed with her knowledge of the Gospel. She had no need to pause, search for Scriptural passages, and read them; she had them already memorized. Wasn't it amazing what a little love and kindness could do for a person whom you had written off as deformed and maybe a little crazy? Later Arthur telephoned to express cautious optimism. He was reluctant to believe anything could go right where that woman was concerned, but it looked as if the plan might work. Unless you saw her, Arthur said, you couldn't believe how good she could look all dressed up and with her hair curled—like Cinderella, a beauty out of the ashes, and so forth. Sherman was charmed. He was already thinking of pushing Rendella toward some kind of simple job—perhaps work at the welfare storehouse or at the Deseret Industries thrift store. Exhilaration came over him and, with it, a sense of gratitude. He always won, but he recognized that he had help far beyond his own abilities.

Early the next Sunday morning Sherman had a telephone call from Arthur. "Things don't look so good," Arthur said in a depressed voice. "I'm afraid maybe it's going to fall to pieces."

"What's going to fall to pieces?"

"It looks like one Sunday is about all Rendella Kranpitz is good for."

"Dang it, Art, you don't have enough faith!"

"I don't know if my faith has anything to do with it. She doesn't look like a person who intends to stick with her bargains."

"For heaven's sake, tell me what's happened."

"She's been on the streets most of the week. And when she disposed of some of that trash, like she promised she would, well, guess what? She called in the opposition."

"The opposition?"

"The Salvation Army truck. You know, instead of calling in the Deseret Industries truck."

"What difference does it make? It all goes to the poor, doesn't it?"

"It just goes to show you what kind of person she is. If she can figure out a way to dig you, she will."

"That doesn't sound so bad, brother," Sherman said, trying to pitch his voice at an enthusiastic level. "Let's go forward with this plan. A few setbacks don't mean anything."

"It's today I'm worried about."

"You mean she won't teach her Sunday School class?"

"Oh, she won't miss that, not on your life. The problem is that yesterday Sister Melchoir and Sister Jacobs went over to help her do her hair. Can you imagine the sacrifice it is for those ladies, with all their kids, to get dressed up on Saturday afternoon and go over to Rendella's for an hour? And she ran them off. She said, What's the matter; you don't think I look so good the way I am, huh? She called them names you wouldn't believe."

"Shall I go to her class today?"

"Would you do that, Sherman? That would sure be great. If you're there, maybe she'll be decent."

A little before the classes were scheduled to begin, Sherman went up the stairs of the meetinghouse, turned down a corridor, and came to the room assigned to Rendella's class. He took a seat at the back. Within a few minutes three couples filed in—the Smiths, the Dinwoodys, and the Horrups. All of them smiled at Sherman and spoke a respectful greeting. The men came to the back for a moment and shook his hand. They all appeared a little resigned, yet hopeful and full of good will. The rank and file of the church, Sherman thought appreciatively, were excellent people—always willing to meet new challenges.

Rendella Kranpitz came in. Sherman shuddered, closed his eyes, then took a second look. Men's shoes, unlaced, clattered on her feet; a vile bag of a dress fluttered around her bony frame; her hair sprouted from her scalp like Swiss chard or turnip tops. Her arms were filled with books—the Scriptures, a lesson manual, sermons by some of the general authorities of the church. She set the books on the table at the front of the room and surveyed the class.

"Where's Brother and Sister Brown?" Rendella asked in a tone of accusation. At that moment the door opened and the couple entered. "There isn't anything so crude and unrefined as busting into a class late," Rendella said. "Can't you come on time?"

The tardy couple murmured an apology as they took seats. Looking up, Sister Brown uttered a gasp of surprise. Rendella advanced threateningly toward her. "Maybe you don't think I dress so good." She glared around the room as if to dare anyone else to disapprove.

"Now the lesson." She returned to the side of the table and stood erect on her good leg, maintaining the other leg at tiptoe in the throat of its unlaced shoe. "Our lesson today is on the gathering of Israel. If you are going to gather Israel, you've got to know who you're gathering. So let's see if you know who Issachar was. Who was Issachar?"

The class members looked blank. Sister Dinwoody thumbed through the pages of her lesson manual.

"You won't find it there," Rendella said. "You're just wasting your time. How come you don't read your Scriptures? Issachar is one of the twelve sons of Jacob." She raised her eyes to the ceiling. "Genesis, chapter forty-nine, verse fourteen: Issachar is a strong ass couching down between two burdens." She looked about triumphantly. "I got you on that one, didn't I?"

Rendella shuffled back and forth, as if undecided. Then, leaning against the table, she directed her eyes toward the light fixture on the ceiling and began to recite: "First Chronicles, chapter two: These are the sons of Israel: Reuben, Simeon, Levi, and Judah, Issachar, and Zebulun, Dan, Joseph, and Benjamin, Naphtali, Gad, and Asher. The sons of Judah: Er, and Onan, and Shelah: which three were born unto him of the daughter of Shua the Canaanitess. And Er, the firstborn of Judah, was evil in the sight of the Lord; and he slew him." She went on for ten or fifteen minutes, unfolding the genealogics of the sons of Jacob. She spoke in a high, oratorical voice and without hesitation, as if she read from a prompter projected on the ceiling. Sherman listened intently, trying to appear alert and interested, but the rocking cadence and monotonous sonority of her words lulled him. With winking eyes and slumping shoulders, he teetered toward sleep.

Rendella's hand suddenly slapped down on the tabletop. "Can't you get your sleeping done at home?" she cried out. Sherman's eyes snapped open, but it was not Sherman she had shouted at. Rendella glowered down on Sister Dinwoody in the second row. "You've got the manners of a magpie," Rendella said belligerently. "Now I've forgotten where I was. I'm going to have to go all the way back to the beginning. Our lesson today is on the gathering of Israel. Israel is a word that means the people of God. At first it was the name of the twelve tribes descended from . . ."

Sister Dinwoody rummaged in her purse. Rendella broke off her speech and waited, arms akimbo, with a mock patience until Sister Dinwoody had found her handkerchief. "You just won't listen to anything, will you?" Rendella said. "Well, if you think you know everything, let's see if you know what this Scripture means. Amos, chapter two, verse two: But I will send a fire upon Moab, and it shall devour the palaces of Kirioth: and Moab shall die with tumult, with shouting, and with the sound of the trumpet."

Rendella leaned toward Sister Dinwoody. "So what does that mean?" Sister Dinwoody dabbed at her eyes with her handkerchief. "Sniffling won't help you any," Rendella said. "Maybe you don't think I teach so good."

Tears flowed from Sister Dinwoody's eyes. She got up, crowded past her husband, and made for the door. "No you don't; not on

your dingdong tintype!" Rendella shouted. She seized Sister Dinwoody by the arm. "Nobody gets out of this class till the bell rings."
    Brother Dinwoody leaped up. "Let loose of my wife, you old cat-
fish!" he cried. He shook Rendella until she released her. Rendella
bent over, took off a shoe, and launched an attack upon Brother
Dinwoody. With a roar he grappled with her, but the best he could
manage was to grip her shoulder with one hand while he used the
other to fend off the flailing shoe.
    "Run for it!" Brother Dinwoody shouted. His wife darted out
the door. The other couples, mouths agape, looked about uncertainly. "Get out of here before she kills me!" he yelled.
    "Let her go, for pity's sake," Sherman shouted. "I can handle
this."
    "Sorry it didn't work out better," Brother Dinwoody said as he
made for the door.
    Rendella stood panting like an animal at bay. Sherman came for-
ward slowly and deliberately, swollen with a magnificent wrath.
Rendella dropped her shoe and with astounding speed lunged
through the door and disappeared beyond the turn in the corridor.
    Coming down the stairs into the foyer of the meetinghouse, Sher-
man met Arthur. Arthur eyed Rendella's abandoned shoe, which
Sherman held in his hand, and said in awe, "What happened,
Sherm? I sure hope Brother and Sister Dinwoody don't apostatize."
    "Go after them and cool them off," Sherman snapped.
    "I don't think I want to get involved in it," Arthur said, backing
away. "Maybe you ought to go talk to them."
    "I said go after them and cool them off. You're bishop, aren't
you?"
    "Well, no," Arthur said. "I resign for sure this time. I've had it
up to here with this business."
    "You can't resign. You were called by inspiration, and by golly
you'll get released by inspiration, which I haven't had any of on the
subject of your release."
    "Disfellowship me if you want to," Arthur said gloomily. "I
can't take any more of this stress."
    "Suffering salamanders, Art!" Sherman roared. "Why do you
have to turn belly up on me every time I get a crisis?"

"I just wasn't cut out to be a bishop. Especially in a ward with Rendella Kranpitz."

"OK, OK, I get your message. You shut up about resigning, and I take over that woman. She's a stake problem now. We'll declare her house a non-ward territory. Now where is she? I'm going to lean on her so hard she won't know up from down."

Sister Horrup informed Sherman that Rendella was cowering in the ladies' rest room in the back wing of the meetinghouse. Sherman stode down the darkened corridor and pounded on the door with Rendella's shoe.

"Rendella Kranpitz, you come out of there," he commanded. There was no response. He pounded and shouted louder. At last he shouted, "I'm counting to ten and then I'm coming in after you. One. Two. Three. Four. Five. Six . . ." The door opened a crack, and an eye gleamed in the dim light.

"Well," Sherman said, a little more calmly, "you sure messed things up royally, didn't you?"

"Yes, sir."

"The best chance you ever had to do something decent, and you spit all over it, didn't you?"

"Yes, sir."

"We are going to give you one more chance. The whole works. And if you mess it up this time, you know what I'm going to do?"

"No, sir."

"I'm going to excommunicate you. You won't be able to go to church anymore. And when you die, you'll go to the telestial kingdom. And you'll never get out. Forever and ever." He smacked his palm with the heel of the shoe. "Now you shape up! Got that?"

"Yes, sir."

"And you get this straight, too. Sherman Colligan never quits. If you misbehave, I'll hunt you down personally. And you're going to get rid of the rest of the trash in your house this week. All of it."

"Yes, sir."

"You're going to let the sisters come over and get you lined up with some decent dresses and a nice hairdo. And you're going to teach a class next Sunday. But you're going to do it right. Just like you did last Sunday. Got that?"

"Yes, sir."

"OK. Take this abominable shoe and go home."

Sherman spent the afternoon reorganizing the rehabilitation of Rendella Kranpitz. For hours he was on the telephone in his office in the stake center. Outside a storm had begun; looking out his office window from time to time, Sherman saw the thick, jostling swirl of snowflakes. Ordinarily he would have watched with tranquil satisfaction, but during this long afternoon he was on edge, still unnerved and disgusted with himself for having spoken abruptly to his good friend Arthur, and for having threatened Rendella with such anger. Love and firmness? It seemed rather that the rehabilitation of this woman might degenerate into fire and brimstone. With that thought, fresh determination came to Sherman. He would personally see to it that the loving pattern of the Gospel would prevail. He decided to call people from all wards in the stake, with the exception of the fifth ward, which could be considered already to have done its duty in this matter. He telephoned a score of people—the individuals who would assist in his project and, of course, their bishops, whose support and approval were vital. When evening had come and Sherman stepped out into the storm, he felt at peace. He could take a moment to appreciate the luminous gyrations of the snowflakes beneath the streetlights. None of the good people he had called seemed half-hearted or doubtful. Once again he felt sure his project would succeed.

Sherman drove home in the snowy darkness, parked in his garage, and tramped along the walk to the front entrance. Celia had turned on the porchlight for him; its rays created an iridescent aura among the floating snowflakes.

And there, sitting on his doorstep, deposited upon a salad plate a little larger than a saucer, was a human stool—a small, looped mound of fresh human excrement.

For a moment Sherman stood transfixed. Then his eyes fell upon tracks in the snow. Though they were half-obliterated, he knew that shuffling foot could belong only to Rendella Kranpitz. Sherman picked up the plate and hid it beneath the drooping branches of a shrub. He shook the snow from his hat and went into the house.

"Hello, sweetheart," Celia said, giving him a kiss. "Isn't it a fine night?"

"Um, yes, a fine night," Sherman mumbled as she helped him take off his overcoat.

"There are sandwiches and soup in the kitchen," she said. "If you want to hurry and wash your hands, Randy is still at the table. You could eat with him."

"Right, good idea. That would be great. I'll hurry," Sherman said. But when he had gotten into the bedroom and had taken off his suitcoat, he sat on the bed, feeling strangely disoriented and removed from reality. It seemed as if nothing in the world was very important. He wondered how long a man could continue in intensive combat without breaking. He remembered having read that some soldiers held up for years; that cheered him for a moment. He reminded himself that Sherman Colligan never quit. There was no reason why he should lose his nerve because of a frail, demented little woman. There was a godly purpose for the affliction which had come to him and his stake—there had to be. His testimony, his sanity depended upon it. Rendella Kranpitz was obviously not a run-of-the-mill test, an ordinary, everyday trial. She was an epic probe, an examination of heroic proportions. Nonetheless, Sherman took out his wallet and looked at his pocket calendar. When his wife came in, she found him still trying to calculate how long it would be until he had served the normal term of a stake president and might expect to be released.

The Canyons of Grace

One summer Arabella Gurney worked as a member of an excavation team at an Anasazi site in the canyon country of Utah. The dig was situated on a small promontory half-encircled by the meandering wash of a broad canyon. To the north were high ridges and the blue Abajo Mountains. South and west the canyon country opened. Its chopped, tilted plains, marked by the red rock of buttes, monoliths, and mesas, ran to the distant rim of the world. In this benign wilderness Arabella found a growing courage for translating her seditious thoughts into an irreversible act. She could remember that, hardly five years earlier, she had thought God loved to bless his children; now she believed his subtle purpose was to demean them.

Arabella was in the kiva on a Saturday morning, working carefully with a tiny pick and brush to unearth a ceremonial dish. Looking up, she saw Franklin's feet dangling against the masonry of the kiva wall. He sat at the edge of the excavation, smiling down like a satyr, his curly hair matted with dust and his bare chest marked by muddy rivulets of sweat.

"I'm coming down," he said, eyeing the ladder.

"There isn't any room," Arabella said. She stood and put a hand on his boot. "Your feet are too big."

He lifted his leg and examined the ponderous boot. "Well, you come up here and sit by me."

When she had seated herself on the rim of the kiva, she reached out and scraped a fingernail along his muddy shoulder. "Utter dirt. You have the hygienic habits of a ground squirrel."

"That dirt," he said proudly, "is the result of a single morning of trenching." He stretched his arm into a right angle and flexed a muscle. "The essence of the male. You may feel it if you want to. Once only."

She pinched his arm vigorously. "Your muscle gives. Maybe it's just water and fat."

"My strength is marvelous, considering what we're getting to eat lately," he said. "The others can't cook worth a damn. The only decent food this camp has had was during the week you and I did the cooking."

"Chiefly me, as I recall."

"Well, yes. I made policy, you carried it out."

"Which means you sat in a camp chair and popped a dishtowel at my behind while I cooked the sausages and eggs."

"I was engaged in creative thought," Franklin said, scratching his head. "I keep wondering where I'd be now if I had minded my old father and had kept out of this pauper's field of anthropology. I have a talent for engineering. I have in mind a project for making alcohol from the juniper berries out there in all those canyons."

"Have you thought of harnessing buzzard power?" Arabella asked, looking up toward a bird floating in the distant sky.

Disdaining her comment, he went on. "I'm looking for a dissertation topic, but there isn't a good one around here. I want to cause an upheaval in anthropology. Maybe I could show that *Homo sapiens* evolved in the Americas."

"Yes, and maybe you could show that Anasazi mythology was piped in on cable TV."

"Lord, you don't take me seriously," Franklin protested. "That's what comes of a fellow being the camp wit and trying to keep everybody's spirits up. When it's time for serious talk, nobody believes him."

Then abruptly, before Arabella could say more, he added, "How come you and me don't set up my little tent across the wash and sleep together?"

A minor tremor of triumph ran through Arabella. She had intuited this moment, had willed it, from the day she had recognized that Franklin was honoring her with the lion's share of his banter.

Unmarried and thirty, she had a flat belly and trim thighs; she wore the standard camp dress of boots, jeans, and halter; each morning she combed her hair into a long tail and tied it at the nape of her neck. She found herself extraordinarily attracted to Franklin's black, curly hair, undisciplined even after combing, his ruddy cheeks and chin, his perpetual smile of satiric good humor. Franklin was garrulous, inveterately drawn to any incongruity, and abounding in appetites. He seemed to be limitlessly educated. He was an unquestioning believer in science and had, in Arabella's judgment, a kind of secular innocence, an enviable ability to suppose that whatever he did was good.

Three ancient cottonwoods spread over the tents and tables of the camp. Directly across the wash from the camp was a hillock covered by sagebrush where Arabella supposed Franklin meant to pitch his tent. It seemed an excessively public place. She had imagined that making love with him would be an occasional matter, something done spontaneously and passionately in the privacy of a remote ravine. Despite an abundance of irreverent talk in the camp, she had seen no pairing off among the graduate students. As for Dr. Muhlestein, he seemed asexual; he puffed stolidly on his pipe, completely absorbed in the plotting and cataloging of the dig and its artifacts. Sleeping in Franklin's tent struck Arabella, on this first consideration, as a too casual, too public declaration of her concupiscence; yet the offer was not something she could let slip by.

"How about it?" Franklin said. "Let's bust out of the dorm tents. Jack snores anyhow."

"Look what courting has come to!" Arabella said. "All you have in mind is getting away from Jack's snoring."

"You want romance? OK, here's a poem: Arabella, Arabella, I'm sure glad you ain't a fella."

"That stinks."

"Arabello, Arabello, you have turned my heart to Jell-O."

"Knock it off."

Franklin stretched out his hand, opened his mouth pretentiously, and bellowed out lines from *La Traviata*. When he stopped, he said, "That was dedicated to my new tentmate."

"Whom you have just killed with an overdose of decibles."

"I continue with a catalog of your charms. You are healthy, you
have pearly white teeth, you are descended from sturdy pioneer
stock. It would be an honor to go to bed with a daughter of the Utah
pioneers."

"And you," she retorted, "are descended from the prince of
darkness. You are the very essence of perversity."

A gratified smile came over Franklin's face. "An apt description.
But let's not digress from praises of your splendid person. There is
about you a mathematical perfection which demonstrates that the
human gene has a passion for geometry. I draw lines from here to
here to here"—his finger traced imaginary lines between her navel
and the points where her halter covered her nipples—"and, voilà,
we find a perfect equilateral triangle. A marvel of nature!" He
leaned back and squinted to get perspective, then made as if to
measure the triangle with the span of his hand.

"Keep your lewd hands off me."

"Lewd! Reverent would be a better word. Besides, lubricity and
lasciviousness are the oil of the living engine: they keep society
renewed. The next generation does not come from a cabbage patch,
as you may have thought."

He placed his hand over her mouth to stifle her reply. "Stop,
cease, desist!" he said. "The camp jester is herewith banished; it is
Franklin speaking to you. I knew from the first time I saw you that it
would be easy to fall in love with you."

Arabella eyed him dubiously. "I would rather not hear things like
that."

"What do you want to hear?"

"Love is a word that doesn't clarify anything."

"OK, no more about it," he agreed. "Is it all right, then? Shall I
set up my tent tonight?"

"Not tonight. Next week."

"Next week! Let's compromise. Tomorrow."

"Wednesday."

"Day after tomorrow."

"OK," she said. "Day after tomorrow."

Franklin shook his head in perplexity. "The whims of the female
sex!" He elevated his eyes. "O Heaven, observe my patience in

the face of ignoble treatment.''

"You'll be struck down for blasphemy," she said.

When Franklin left, Arabella returned to her work on the floor of the kiva. She bent again over the emerging ceremonial dish. Ordinarily, as she pried at the resisting soil and brushed away its loosened particles, she fell into a harmony with the artifact; she found a rhythm, an unthinking cooperation of her attentive eyes, her accurate hands, her tenacious will. In certain mystical moments she became a creator, a sculptor who from the melded mass of soil and buried artifact declared the original shape of the past and returned it to the dawning moment of the present. But on this day, her mind taken up by Franklin's proposition, she could not find the rhythm of her work. She circled about the fact of her courage: it was incredible that she had held steady, had been calm, a little coy, and able to parry his banter. Fragments of passionate fantasy jostled in her mind. She saw herself with Franklin. They stood in the middle of the wash late at night, watched by the bright stars. He embraced her, unfastened her halter and fondled her breasts, as men were pleased to do.

"I have this book," she said to him. "It says that when a bride and groom go to bed for the first time . . .''

"Who's a bride and groom?" Franklin protested.

"According to this book, which I bought last spring in Salt Lake City, and which, really, you might want to read—"

"Hell, Arabella," Franklin groaned, "this isn't any time to be talking about a book. I know what to do."

"I mean that when a woman has had no experience, the man is cautioned to go easy. The first time."

"God, you're a virgin," Franklin said with reverence for the gift she was giving him.

Abandoning her reserve, she drove her fantasy to lush intensity. They lay naked on top of sleeping bags in Franklin's tent. They explored each other completely and ardently, and then, making love, they triumphed.

In the floor of the kiva near where Arabella squatted was a small, rock-lined excavation. It was a *sipapu,* a representation of the passage through which, in Anasazi creation myths, the first human beings had passed into the light of day from the dark, gestating caverns of the earth's womb. It was, as Dr. Muhlestein had said one evening at supper, an Anasazi fertility symbol, a celebration of the human vagina. Arabella was both attracted and repelled by the *sipapu*. It looked like no part of the female body, yet at times, as she had worked in the kiva, it had served as an aphrodisiac, impelling her erotic fantasies. Hidden away in this ancient place of pagan worship, connected to the inscrutable earth in wild holiness, it seemed to warrant rebellious desire. But at other times the scared *sipapu* was a reproach, and now, as Arabella's mood shifted, she remembered grimly that her ovaries, her womb, her vagina were not hers to dispose of in pleasure; they belonged to God, a sacred territory which Arabella held in virginal stewardship.

She remembered a night in May less than a month before she had come to the canyon country. She had been home from the university for the weekend. Her mother had called her into the kitchen for milk and cookies. Her father was there, too, and the three of them, dressed in bathrobes, talked aimlessly. After a while her father turned off the kitchen lights to show the moonlight in the backyard. Through the screen of the patio door they saw, washed in white, the lawn, the flower borders, the oak thicket, the tangle of rose and pyracantha bushes at the edge of the property.

In an apologetic tone her mother said, "It seems like a mother shouldn't be asking for promises when her daughter is thirty."

"Promises?"

"Smell those plum blossoms from up the way," her mother said. "We used to walk up to Jorey's orchard with you kids. That stopped when they built the subdivision above us. We ought to drive around sometime and see the trees, I guess."

"They're relics," her father said. "Jorey doesn't cultivate his trees anymore. They just grow wild."

"What kind of promises?" Arabella insisted.

Her mother reached across the table and stroked the back of her hand. "Forgive me for being so fearful. Please promise me that you will never be with a man until you have prayed to see if it is all right."

"To be with a man?"

"I mean to have an intimacy."

"To have sex," Arabella said belligerently.

"Yes," her mother said. "Because if it is right, you will know it after you have prayed."

"That seems like an odd thing to say to me," Arabella said. "I'm not thinking of getting married."

"I wish you liked somebody enough to get married," her mother said. "That Jerald Henson was a nice man."

"Gol, Mom, let's not go into that again. I wouldn't want him under any circumstance."

"Well, never mind. What I wanted to say is that, with the loose way things are in the world, anybody needs protection. If you pray about it, you won't fall."

Arabella's mother went to the refrigerator, returning with a container. She set her husband's glass into the strip of moonlight on the table and poured him more milk. An accusation had been made, Arabella saw; yet she could not maintain the indignation she had felt when her mother had first spoken. She was frightened to acknowledge the uncanny precision with which her parents had intuited her intention.

"Chastity is a serious thing," her mother said.

"I know."

"Even married people have to be careful. I mean with each other. You have to have a consideration for each other in the way you dress, and you shouldn't do things that will provoke each other before the Spirit tells you it is proper to make love."

Arabella held the lip of the ceremonial dish with firm fingers while she pried a pebble from its underside; then she paused to trowel the gathered detritus into a bucket. Caught in the mood of that May night, she had worked in the kiva with a mechanical inattention. She recognized now that the cookies and milk had not been coincidental; her parents, usually reticent, had been coerced into an extreme action. She had not thought of them for days in this hot, sun-filled wilderness, but now, in the aftermath of Franklin's proposition, she again felt their drastic pull. She recognized that they had believed her to be on the edge of disaster: the unprecedented allusion to their own intimate life and the embarrassing presence of her father were evidence of that. Arabella could not remember having ever heard from either of them the slightest admission that they knew each other sexually, though the fact was visible enough in their ten children. Her father and mother were amazingly alike: reverent in the extreme, scrupulous in keeping the commandments, and doubtful of their salvation. Arabella loathed them for their subservience, yet she also loved them, needed their approval, and understood perfectly that God was to be feared. She sat back for a moment on the floor of the kiva to relieve the ache of her squatting legs. She remembered the grieving good-by which had hung in the air of the moon-spotted kitchen. Again she wavered, had second thoughts, and wondered whether she could reconcile herself to God's will. And again she marveled at her unrelenting, desperate compulsion to persist in her freedom—to the point of perdition, if necessary.

That night—it being a Saturday—she and Franklin went to Blanding with Magnus and Becky. As a concession to town, she put on lipstick and wore a chambray shirt. Franklin gestured her into the back seat of Magnus's car, and while the vehicle sped along the road leading from the dig to the highway he sat close to her, took her hand in both of his, and toyed abstractly with her fingers. They listened as Magnus and Becky, shouting over the clatter of gravel against the fenders, gossiped about things at camp. As Magnus turned the car onto the highway, Franklin placed in Arabella's lap a small bundle wrapped in a faded green towel.

"It's Christmas," he said. "Please take note of the gaily colored wrapping on this package."

"For me?"

"A gift. However, I would appreciate the return of the towel, since it's the only clean one I've got."

Arabella unraveled the folds of the towel. A smaller package, wrapped in white stationery, emerged. In a moment a flint spear head fell into her hand.

"Gol, a projectile point!"

"It's from Tabeguache Canyon," Franklin said. "Notice how sharp it is." He pointed to the serration which numerous minute flutings had formed along the edges of the long, thin point.

"I never saw a Tabeguache point before."

"It's pre-Anasazi. The real thing," Franklin said proudly.

For a moment her eyes lighted with a covetous esteem; then disappointment crossed her face. "I couldn't take it," she said, handing the point to Franklin. "It's too valuable."

"No, really," Franklin insisted. "It's for you."

She shook her head and refused to take the point in her hands.

"For crying out loud," he said incredulously, "I want you to have it. Don't you like it?"

Reluctantly Arabella took the point again. She stroked it with her fingers and said, "It's beautiful. I never had anything like it before."

She handed it forward to Becky, who examined it and held it out for Magnus to see. As Becky returned the point, Arabella was troubled, not so much by the public recognition of her attachment to Franklin as by the pleasure she took in that recognition. There was a disturbing comfort in the press of Franklin's shoulder against hers. When, a moment before, he had squeezed her hand—a gesture of affection which she had seen exchanged a hundred times by her father and mother—she had involuntarily squeezed his hand in return. She saw within herself an alarming impulse for domesticity, a desire for stability and belonging. For a moment, turning the cool flint point in her fingers, she felt deceived. She had supposed that Franklin, who was divorced and seemed the essential man of the world, would have had enough of entanglements. She had imagined all along a condition of friendly fornication between them, a congenial accommodation of simple lust. To burden their relationship with affection, protectiveness, or loyalty seemed a corruption of it. Beyond the expression of her sexuality she had relied on a single stark motivation for going to bed with Franklin: it was to be an act of defiance, a thousand-megaton blow against the conformities of her previous life.

In Blanding they went for a hamburger at Minnie's Good Eats, a little cafe with grimy walls, chipped counters, and missing floor tiles. They settled into a booth and called a greeting to Minnie, who, after she had poured a glass of water for a man at the counter, waved an obese arm toward them. The man turned to scrutinize them. He wore ancient trousers of worsted wool, a blue shirt, and a narrow yellow tie. His head bristled with clipped grey hair. Thick, steel-rimmed spectacles magnified his eyes. Having scanned the room, he let his eyes rest on Arabella.

"Who's that old coot?" Magnus said.

"Don't fret about these rural types," Franklin said. "You can't keep up with them."

"Let's drive down to Moab tomorrow and go to a show," Becky said.

"God!" Magnus snorted. "I'd rather spend the day in camp. Let's go to Cortez and find a bar with some loud music."

When the waitress came to the booth, Franklin said, "Gimme a beer, a beer, a beer." He lowered his voice successively and dropped his curly head onto the table.

Magnus laughed and said, "Another victim of science and the glory of the University of Utah expeditionary force. I'll take a beer, too. And a hamburger. And a big order of fries. In fact, make that two hamburgers."

"We don't have a license to sell beer," the waitress said. "You can drink it here if you want to bring your own."

"Oh, hell!" Magnus said.

"Make my order the same as his," Franklin said. Then he shoved Magnus from the booth. "See you ladies in a minute," he called as he followed Magnus from the cafe. "We'll bring you back some beer."

"You're Janet, aren't you?" Arabella said to the waitress. "Do you remember us? We were here two weeks ago."

"I remember," Janet said. "I knew you were working that dig west of here, but I didn't know which university you were from."

Janet took the orders to Minnie in the kitchen; then, untying her apron, she disappeared through a back door. The man with the bristling grey hair and the steel-rimmed spectacles rose and walked to the side of the booth near Arabella. Beads of sweat stood on his forehead. He leaned close and fixed his eyes upon hers. "I don't

know your name," he said. "That doesn't matter any. You don't
know my name, either, but you will. God has a promise for you.
He's got an eye on you."
    Becky tried to stand up in the booth. "Listen, dude, beat it. We
don't have to listen to that kind of bullshit."
    The old man turned on Becky. "Sit down, girl. I didn't ask
anything of you." Becky sat back with a look of stupefaction on her
face. The old man returned his eyes to Arabella. "I'm a prophet,"
he said. "I know God. In fact, I've seen Him. Sister, He has set you
apart to be my wife."
    Janet came from the back room and stood at the end of the
counter. "I've got eight wives," the old man went on. "They take it
an honor to be my wife." He walked to a table, pulled away a chair,
and brought it to the booth. "Come out of there," he said to
Arabella. "Sit right here. I'm going to ordain you."
    Arabella looked helplessly at Becky. "Sister, you come," he said.
She sat in the chair. He put his hands on her head, pressed heavily,
and prayed: "God Almighty, by the authority Thou hast bestowed
on me, the head of Thy only one and single true church, I lay my
hands on the head of this sister . . ." He paused. "What's your
name?" Arabella was silent. "What's your name?" he burst out indignantly.
    "Arabella Gurney."
    "I lay my hands on the head of this sister, Arabella Gurney," he
continued, "and I consecrate her unto the duty and elevation of
wifehood unto Thy servant, Thy prophet, even myself. Amen."
    Anxiety paralyzed Arabella. For a moment she had believed her-
self on the verge of a terrible surrender. She had scarcely registered
the meaning of the old man's words; they had merged in her ears as
intonations of fervor, threat, and revelation. As his heavy hands
lifted from her scalp, electric sensations surged in her belly and
thighs. She pulsed with an uncanny recognition. Though he was a
man she had never seen before in her life, she found him familiar
and felt in his behavior a perfect harmony with an unthought expec-
tation.
    The old man stood back, gazing at her. "Sister, your sins are
forgiven. If you have been doing unholy things with one of those

young men, or any other, I don't care what your sin is, you're clean.
I can do that. What I bind on earth is bound in heaven, and what I
loosen on earth is loosened in heaven."
He turned to Janet and took her arm. "Let's go," he said. At the
door he paused, turned, and came back to Arabella. "I don't force
anyone. God gives free agency to everybody. But don't take too
long. When your mind is made up, tell Janet. You know where to
find her. Or you can go daytime to the Texaco station in Monticello.
Ask for Grant. Don't take too long."
As he spoke, the door from the street opened and Franklin and
Magnus entered. Franklin stood a moment, his mouth agape. Shifting a paper sack from one arm to the other, he burst out, "What the
hell is going on here?"
The old man paused before Franklin, his lips puckered in scornful
distaste. "I can smell damnation on some men. It smells worse than
rot," he said. "But I've got nothing against you boys. Neither one
of you." His eyes swung to include Magnus. "You never knew any
better. I'm making you an offer, the best of your whole life. Come
out of Babylon. If you want to get off the track to destruction, let
me know. But I don't force anybody. You come or you don't come.
That's up to you."
"Who is that old son of a bitch?" Franklin exploded as the door
closed behind Janet and the old man.
"Reuben Millring," Minnie said, coming from the kitchen with
platters of hamburgers and French fries. "Janet ain't his wife; she's
Grant's wife. Grant is his son. But Reuben runs everything. They
obey him like a king." Having served the orders, Minnie returned to
lean against the counter. She picked up an ashtray and, rotating it
through her fingers, spoke to Arabella. "Maybe I got no business
intruding. We're more or less strangers, but if I was you, I would
sure get out of this country."
"God, it's scary!" Becky said. "He says he's got eight wives and
Arabella is going to be the next one. He made her sit in that chair
while he put his hands on her head and said a prayer."
Franklin strode angrily to the door and peered out. "I wish I'd
known that while he was still here. I'd have knocked that old
bastard through the wall."

"He's got people all over the Four Corners country," Minnie continued. "They worship him, and they'll kill for him. People laugh when I say that; they say, Aw, he's just an old religious fanatic, he don't do no real harm. But I totaled up one time all the names I heard from one person or another that has died because of that old man, and there was eleven of them."

"This is the twentieth century, for God's sake!" Franklin said.

"I happen to know for a fact that he had his brother Zachariah killed," Minnie said. "They was co-prophets for years. I used to see Zachariah at least once a week, and now, by God, he's gone and no one knows where he is. But I know, because Sandy Deams at Wentworth's trading post told me, and I believe him. Zachariah and Reuben quarreled over who had the most direct line to God, and a guy named Ramsay killed Zachariah. Reuben told him to. It's blood atonement. Ever hear of that? Just get Janet going on it sometime if you want to hear something to chill you down. That ain't all. There was a couple, a man and a woman who wasn't married to each other. I never knew them, but Sally Riggs from Mexican Hat knew for a fact what happened to them. They belonged to the Church of Sacrifice, which is the name of Rueben's church. They got to messing with each other, which was wrong because they was married to other people. When it came out, their throats was cut and they were buried somewhere off the road to the Goosenecks of the San Juan."

Returning to the camp that night, Arabella let her eyes drift aimlessly across the scenes and objects flashing by the headlights—a yellow sandstone cliff, the gnarled skeleton of an ancient juniper, a scampering rat. She leaned against Franklin, responding perfunctorily to his kisses and tolerating his caressing hands. Her thoughts revolved violently around the image of the stern old man. With each mile she remembered more clearly what he had said and done, and she was haunted again by the feeling that he was no mystery to her, that she knew him perfectly well. Arabella had not needed Minnie's explanation to convince her that Reuben Millring was an agent of Judgment, a predator upon the sinful who came into his power. He had said that he could smell damnation. Arabella could smell it, too. All her life it had been her gift to sense the distant reality of perdition, to feel it in the soles of her feet, like seismic vibrations from deep in the earth, or to rub its debris between her fingertips, like fine dust drifted by a windstorm upon windowsills and tabletops. Suddenly, despite the darkness in the car, Arabella felt herself detected, looked upon, scrutinized. She could not now think of any reason for having agreed to Franklin's proposition. The concupiscent tryst toward which they were moving was lethal; God would not fail to give it his closest, most angry attention. She could not possibly go through with it. Pressing helplessly against Franklin as the car, rounding a curve, unbalanced her, she recognized her immeasurable, despicable cowardice.

Arabella awoke before dawn the next morning. She heard sounds of sleep from the cots where Narna and Becky lay and, beyond the walls of the tent, the leaves of the cottonwoods stirring in the breeze of the waning night. Arabella thought of a remote canyon she had found in one of her hikes and felt a hunger for its seclusion.

At midmorning she left camp. On the ridge west of the dig she looked back and saw Franklin panting up the slope behind her.

"I want to come along," he said. "Is that OK?"

"I'm going a long way."

"That's all right. I'm for it."

For an hour they hiked along ridges, through arroyos, across broad slopes. The sandy soil over which they walked bore sparse clumps of bending yellow grass, linked spiny disks of prickly pear, and groves of juniper and pinyon.

"Good Lord, how far are you going?" Franklin asked as she paused to look at a flower.

"About an hour more."

"With all due respect to the civilized sport of hiking," Franklin said, "this is really rather boring."

"Maybe if you went back you could catch the others before they leave for town. I'll be OK alone."

"They're gone," he said with disgust. "Let's go back and play chess."

"This is a pretty flower," she said, bending to sniff it.

He squatted by her and fondled the plant. "I should have brought my flower guide. This belongs to the *Penstemon* family." Franklin sidestepped until his hip and shoulder rested against hers. "This feels good. A little tactile involvement. Premature infants die without it, and grizzled archeologists languish for lack of it."

"You are about to push me over," Arabella complained.

"Excellent! Let's make love. We could find a nice shady place."

"Don't you think human acts have an ultimate consequence?"

"What is this—a lecture on ethics?"

"I mean that I believe in sin."

Laughing loudly, Franklin fell back into the dirt. "Lordy, so do I! Sin is a terrible thing. Let's commit one right now."

"If sin is real," she said, "it carries inherent risks. What I need is a table showing the specific gravity of all possible sins. Since you know mathematics, give me a calculus for computing the risk of a given sin—for example, the sin you are asking me to commit with you in these pinyons."

"Let's not worry about the calculus until we have committed the sin," he protested. "Shall we proceed with it?"

Arabella stood and walked to the projecting bough of a pinyon. She examined the needles carefully. "I wondered if this would be a single-leaf pinyon. But it isn't."

"*Pinus monophylla* is found in scattered places in western Utah and eastern Nevada," Franklin said. "You'll find only *Pinus edulis* here—the double leaf."

"Gosh," she exclaimed with mock respect. She did not yet have the courage to tell him that she had changed her mind about sleeping in his tent. "Taxonomy is a constipating discipline. Nonetheless, I appreciate the precise naming of the species of pinyon. Distinct speciation is one of the evidences of a divine creation."

"Divine creation, my foot," Franklin muttered. "Don't you know that biologists can't even agree on what a species is?"

"Please give me a formal argument that God doesn't exist. I would like to hear why I shouldn't believe in God."

"OK," Franklin said. "There are six major arguments. Number one is the awkwardness of the creation theory you just mentioned. If you assume over a million species in the animal world alone, can you imagine how busy—"

"I've heard all those arguments," she interrupted. "What I need is a sure testimony, a revelation. I want to be ravished, burst in upon, enveloped in flames of the Spirit testifying that God doesn't exist."

"Let's pray about it," Franklin said. He knelt in the sandy soil, pressed his palms together, and tucked his hands under his chin. "Father, we supplicate Thee this day in behalf of one Arabella Gurney, doubter, that Thou wouldst—"

"The problem is," she said, growing brave at last, "that I can't sleep in your tent."

He sat back on his heels, picked up a pinyon twig, and examined it with an abstract curiosity. When he looked at her his face was utterly sober. "I was counting on it," he said quietly.

"I really do believe in God," she said. "I know it's absurd, but I believe. And I'm afraid."

"It's that old son of a bitch at Minnie's cafe," Franklin sighed dismally. "I knew he would screw things up."

"At least he reminded me," Arabella admitted. "He's so strange. He's like someone I might have known in my pre-existence."

"Well, nothing good is happening here," Franklin said. "Let's go wherever it is you're going."

"One thing more—I can't keep the Tabegauche point."

"Sure you can keep it. I gave it to you."

"No. I wouldn't feel right about it."

"It wasn't an engagement ring, and it wasn't a bribe to buy me an easy lay. I gave it to you because I wanted you to have it. And you damn well better keep it."

But she was already hiking onward. She walked without pause until, nearly an hour later, she and Franklin emerged from the trees upon the rim of a high plateau. She led the way along the rim, across a sloping watershed, and down a ravine into a deep, narrow canyon. A plunge pool, thirty feet across and filled with shimmering water, lay in the slickrock at the head of the canyon. She led Franklin to the edge of the pool and pointed to the nearby canyon wall. A portion of the cliff was marked by a profusion of petroglyphs. Dozens of figures had been tapped into the perpendicular stone in narrow, angular lines.

"This canyon is filled with grace," Arabella said.

"Goddamn!" Franklin muttered.

"They move me like poems," she added.

Some of the figures were abstract. There were zigzag lines, coils, spirals, and circles. Other figures were representational. There was a goat with back-curving horns, a beard, and cloven hooves. A deer-like creature stood above four detached feet, each of which had five toes. A man held a bow from which an arrow had fallen. A large lizard was attached by its forefeet and snout to a recumbent man. Above all the others was a strange, humanoid image topped by a misshapen head from which sprouted three antennae.

"I need to talk," Arabella said, "though I also have an impulse to be hushed. I am awed, reduced to reverence by this place. Isn't there a god here?"

"Sure, a katchina with horns and feathers," Franklin said brightly.

He knelt and idly stirred his fingers in the pool. Very tentatively, with an uncharacteristic caution, he said, "Do you really believe there's a god in this canyon?"

Arabella laughed. "What difference would it make?"

"I don't know. I never met an animist before."

"I'm not an animist," she said, "though sometimes in wild places I have an intuition of holiness. Maybe that is pagan—the worship of a false divinity—and God will hold it against me."

"Christ, what a terrible thing to believe!"

"I have tried to shake it, but I can't. If I let you make love to me, I have stepped further into damnation."

"There isn't any such thing as damnation! That's medieval."

Arabella bent down to inspect a group of ants tugging at the carcass of a black beetle. Her nose wrinkled with distaste as she flipped the beetle with her finger. "When I die, the scavengers will eat me, too. Thinking about it nauseates me. I want to be saved from the wilderness—because if wilderness is the ultimate reality, I will die forever."

"Lord but that's morbid talk!"

"You're not afraid of annihilation?"

"I don't think about it."

"Just as an animal doesn't think about it."

Franklin was stung. "I'm no more an animal than you are."

"The horror lies in the possibility that neither of us is more than an animal. There has to be a God. No one else can save me, though the price He asks is my integrity."

Franklin wandered into the sandy wash which led away down the canyon. "OK, Franklin boy," he muttered, "you just keep your old cool." Whistling, he began to walk. At a point where the wash curved around a protruding fin of rock, he stopped and faced Arabella, who had followed him.

"You don't have to be religious to be decent," he said.

"That's true."

"I'm a decent fellow."

Arabella laughed. "That's doubtful."

"Wouldn't you like to marry a professor?"

"Like Dr. Muhlestein?"

"No. Like me."

Arabella scrutinized him in surprise.

"I'm a professorial bud now in the process of blooming, and I've had enough of the single life."

"Marriage is a violation of the solipsistic self."

Franklin ignored her. "I'm not religious. But that doesn't matter, does it? I don't mind if you are religious if you don't mind if I'm not."

"Gol," she said, "how do I know if I want to marry anyone? How can I see that far down the road?" But she was touched. "Why would you want to marry me?"

"You told me not to say I was in love with you. But I am." They both looked at the toe of his boot, which traced an arc in the sand. "We could get married."

Tears had come to her eyes. "I'm glad you love me," she said.

She took his hand and they went down the wash until they came to a ledge where the canyon terminated, plunging hundreds of feet to another canyon below. Franklin cut a juniper twig, sat on the bank of the wash, and began to whittle. He scowled a little as he concentrated on his whittling. Arabella walked onto the overhanging ledge and sat cross-legged upon the rock. The relief she had sought by coming to this canyon began to creep upon her. The sky overhead was blue and adrift with white clouds. Dark forests of pinyon and juniper covered the land before her. The land rose and fell in broad undulations. It was rifted with canyons and studded with mesas, buttes, and high vertical monoliths standing stark against the country behind. Arabella recognized the wilderness; holiness came over her. She was elevated, amplified, immeasurably reassured. She strained to understand. The holy wild told her she was free. She had never felt so completely, so inviolably herself.

She was breathless to exploit her courage before it fled. She turned to Franklin. He seemed absorbed in his whittling. "If it isn't too late," she began, "if you won't think I'm strange for changing my mind so soon . . ."

Franklin looked up, puzzled and waiting.

"If you want to make love," she said, "I think I would like it here."

Cautious pleasure moved on Franklin's face. "I was serious about getting married."

"Please, can we just let things go for a while?"

"OK," he said.

They undressed, put their clothes on the sand, and lay down together. Images crowded her mind—the steel-rimmed eyes of Reuben Millring, the humanoid petroglyph with antennae sprouting from its head, the carcass of the black beetle, sent scuttling by the flick of her finger, the tear-streaked face of her mother. Arabella resisted the images, allowed none of them to anchor; they drifted, distended, transformed one into another. Franklin finished with startling speed, but Arabella did not mind, feeling a vast relief that the act was complete, her bridges burned, her way decided. She held Franklin tightly upon her, gazing past his head, past the looming walls of the canyon, on into the serene blue of the sky. She did not doubt her damnation. But for the moment, pushing aside her anxiety, she chose to exult in her courage, to relish the taste of her daring.

For many weeks afterward Arabella took shelter in the transient freedom of the wilderness and accepted its bright promises. There was, during those days, an undreamed-of fulfillment, an overbrimming of her perverse joy. She slept in Franklin's tent and found herself possessed by an immense affection for him; like a summer plant, whatever was between them seemed doomed and therefore precious. She asked Franklin to drill a hole into the shank of the Tabegauche spearpoint through which she threaded a nylon cord, and she wore the point as a necklace. Night and day it hung at the base of her brown throat. She did not go to town, and she refused to think about God. In her feelings she had set arbitrary limits to the universe; it was no larger or more significant than this hot, bright wilderness in which she lived. She hiked often in the land around the dig, sometimes with Franklin or others, more often alone.

Hiking alone on a Sunday late in the summer, Arabella saw a rider coming obliquely from behind her. She assumed that the man, who rode one horse and led another, was a cowboy from Blanding. When the clatter of shod hooves on rock warned her that the rider had overtaken her, she turned to say hello. The rider wore a dilapidated Stetson, a soiled white shirt, and brogans instead of boots. He ignored her greeting, reined his horse in, and pulled the other one around until it was between himself and Arabella.

"Get on," he said. "Reuben wants you."

She watched him for a moment, then turned and broke into a run. Shouting and kicking, the rider forced his horses into a gallop and quickly came up behind Arabella, who dodged into a clump of junipers. The rider circled the trees. When Arabella stopped to pant, he leaned from his saddle and tied the unmounted horse to a branch.

"Maybe I don't look like a cowboy," he said, "but I'm going to tell you something. There ain't any better cutting horse in this county than this one I'm riding. When he figures out it's you I'm after, you don't have a chance."

Arabella backed away, putting another tree between herself and the rider.

"Reuben said I had to do whatever it took to bring you along," the man said.

Arabella launched herself into a frantic run. The horse gained on her as she dodged in and out among the trees, and suddenly, anticipating another evasive dart, the horse shouldered into her and knocked her sprawling into the rocks and cactus.

An hour later she and the man rode into a ravine, struck the tracks of a primitive road, and in a few minutes came upon a parked cattle truck. "Here she is," the rider said to a small bald man who climbed from the cab. "I ain't sure she knows just what is going on. She got hit pretty hard. But it wasn't my fault. She ran into the horse when she was dodging."

The bald man helped Arabella dismount and led her to the truck. "Get in there and I'll get you some water," he said. His protruding Adam's apple rippled when he talked.

"I'm not getting in," she said, pulling back.

The rider had dismounted and had pulled down the loading ramp at the rear of the truck. Peering around the corner of the truck bed he said, "You behave. Your chances with Reuben are better if you do. He ain't going to be all that happy about you. I don't know what he wanted with a slut like you in the first place. He counted on you keeping clean. We been watching that camp. We know you been shacked up with that curly-haired fellow."

Arabella got in. The two men loaded the horses, clanged the loading ramp into position, and climbed into the cab. As the rider positioned himself behind the steering wheel Arabella said, "You're Ramsay."

"It don't matter none who I am."

"No harm telling her," the other man said. "I'm Grant and he's Ramsay. He didn't mean to hurt you. We got your best interest to heart." He took up a water jug from the floor and poured a drink for Arabella. He looked at Ramsay. "I want to treat her right," he said. "I got a strong feeling she's going to be Dad's next wife."

"And maybe she won't be, too," Ramsay said. "Look at that spearpoint she's wearing for a necklace. She looks like an Indian."

The truck jolted to the highway, sped westward, then turned north on a gravel road which followed a creek bottom filled with groves of cottonwoods and thickets of willow. The truck rippled over a cattle guard, turned sharply, and entered a village. Ramsay shut off the engine. Dogs barked and children shouted. Houses built of rock, cinderblock, and wood were scattered haphazardly along either side of the meandering creek. Front yards were cluttered by lumber, old crates, and junked automobiles; there were no fences or lawns. Behind the houses stood barns, sheds, and corrals. Crowding close upon the little valley were steep ridges thickly covered by juniper and pinyon.

Grant took Arabella into a large house. A woman came from a dark hall, buttoning her blouse and pushing strands of grey hair into place.

"This is Arabella Gurney," Grant said. The woman nodded, and he left.

"We didn't know when you were coming," the woman said. "I'm Winifred. You're surely most welcome." She motioned Arabella to a sofa and sat down beside her. Rag rugs covered the waxed wood floor. Around the room stood sturdy oak chairs, and there was a table decorated with tiny doilies. On the walls hung ancestral pictures and a portrait of Christ.

Winifred looked wistfully into Arabella's eyes. "I was his first," she said. "He's a wonderful man. He always tells us when another is coming to join our circle."

Winifred touched Arabella's cheek with her fingers; her own cheeks were seamed with minute wrinkles. "You are pretty. Be patient with him. It isn't what a girl dreams about before she is married. People in the world think they have to have their own husbands, as if a husband was something like a necklace or a pair of shoes. But it isn't hard to share. I count myself the most blessed woman. Not every woman has a prophet for a husband. God is among us. You can feel Him every day."

In a moment Winifred led Arabella down the darkened hall and opened a door. "This is your room. It's in the coolest part of the house. Doesn't it get hot in this country! I just don't seem to ever get used to it. I'm from Michigan, you know."

The small room smelled of fresh paint and floor wax. A brass bed stood in the center; a dresser with a mirror filled one corner. A basin and pitcher rested on the dresser.

"Take off those things of yours, if you don't mind," Winifred said. "Reuben won't like them. I'll bring you a dress. My Sally is your size."

Arabella sat on the edge of the bed and looked about in a half-stupor. Her head ached and her back throbbed. She lifted one leg, unlaced the heavy boot, and started to pull it off. Then she paused, dropped her foot without removing the boot, and began to weep. She was appalled to realize how numbly and automatically she had set herself to obey Winifred. Her jeans and boots and faded halter, her brown arms and belly were signs of her identity. If she let anyone take them off or cover them up, who might she be? Despite all that, her resistance faded quickly as Winifred entered the room, sat by her on the bed, and comforted her. Arabella gratefully allowed the older woman to undress her, sponge her with water, and rub her with alcohol.

"You lie and rest now," Winifred said, "and when it is time for supper I'll come help you get into this dress. Don't you think it is pretty?" She held up a cream-colored dress with white collar and cuffs. Before leaving the room Winifred knelt by the bed and pressed her cheek against Arabella's. "Don't feel bad," she said in a yearning voice. "We will love you. You don't know what love is until you have loved a sister wife."

When Winifred brought Arabella to supper, the men and women at the large kitchen table were already into their meal. In the twilight beyond the screened windows crickets chirruped melodically. Winifred seated Arabella next to Reuben, who did not seem to notice her. Reuben tore a large crust from a loaf of bread and spread it thickly with butter. His eyes gave abstract attention to his hand as he knifed the butter from a small crock. He poured milk into his bowl, from which he drank as if it were a cup.

"Your father is Delbert Gurney," he said, handing the loaf of bread to Arabella and pushing the butter and milk toward her. "He's an insurance agent in Bountiful. He's well thought of in those parts."

Arabella looked helplessly at Winifred, who took the loaf from her and cut her a slice. The white collar of Arabella's dress was buttoned high around her neck; her hair was plaited in two long, tight braids.

Reuben went on. "I found out this afternoon that Ezra met your father last week in Murray. Pure accident. He never heard of him before in his life, but in two minutes he knew Delbert Gurney was your dad. It's been on my mind how come God put your father in Ezra's way.''

Reuben chewed his food methodically and waited until he had swallowed to speak again. "There are five hundred of us, more or less. We have churches spread from Hanksville to Durango. Two parties of us are in New Mexico. These people are the Saints. They're doing what God has told them to do. When the fire comes, they'll be safe in these canyons.''

"Ramsay says the Savior will come in five years," said a woman at the end of the table.

"I wish Ramsay would keep out of things he doesn't know anything about," Reuben said. "I haven't been told. How does he know?''

Looking at Arabella, Reuben said, "I'm going to tell you something." He paused and looked again at the woman at the end of the table. "Get some of those green tomato preserves, would you? I could relish a little of them.''

He leaned toward Arabella. "Spencer W. Kimball is a fallen prophet. I testify to you that he is a counselor of Satan. I know that for a fact. Harold B. Lee was an apostate; Joseph Fielding Smith was an apostate. President Taylor was the last man in the Mormon church to have the keys. Things went bad when Wilford Woodruff turned his back on polygamy. Who ever heard of God changing His mind! The true church has gone underground. That's us. In these canyons are the most righteous people on earth. Right here you are closer to God than anywhere else you could be. There aren't many of us. That doesn't bother me any; there never have been many of God's elect. I don't take any glory when I tell you I am the only true prophet on the face of the earth. It's my duty to tell you. My father gave me the keys by the laying on of hands, and his father gave them to him, and he got them from President Taylor.''

Just then a man came in through an outside door. Murmuring to the group, he carried a bucket of milk to the sink, where he stretched a cloth over the rim of the bucket and strained the milk into a pan.

"How are things, Lorenzo?" Reuben said, shifting in his chair to watch.

"Reese's boy says there's a cow in the quicksand in Tambel Canyon."

"Why didn't he get her out?"

"Didn't have a rope."

"These youngsters can't do anything by themselves," Reuben said. "Well, get her out of there. We can't take any more losses on cattle."

As Lorenzo left the kitchen, Reuben returned his eyes to Arabella. "I was thinking from what Ezra says your father must be one of the best men God ever put on earth."

Flushed and confused, Arabella looked at her bowl of milk.

"You're proud of your father and mother, aren't you?"

Arabella gave him a quick, incredulous glance.

"Well, aren't you proud?" Reuben insisted. "You wouldn't do anything to shame them, would you?"

"No," she said, "I wouldn't want to shame them."

"That's right," Reuben said. "Any of us wants to be a credit to our father and mother, don't we?"

Arabella stared down upon the cream-colored fabric of her dress. She pitied her overworked, self-denying father; she ached for her quiet, worried mother. Tears fell fast into her lap.

Reuben set his knife across his bowl, gripped the arms of his chair, and watched Arabella intently. Moment by moment, as the others at the table noticed, the clatter of knives and forks died away and the motion of chewing jaws halted.

"I want to say something to this people," Reuben declared. "William, I want this set in writing. This woman is weeping for her sins. The bitterness of hell has got her. But that isn't the end. This woman is going to be the mother of one of the greatest men in the last days. If she will repent and follow the truth, it will happen. There won't be any failing of it. It's a sure prophecy."

"That's so beautiful," Winifred said, also weeping. "Doesn't that make you feel happy, Arabella?"

"Likely, if you asked your father and mother, they would take us for apostates," Reuben said. "I don't begrudge them for that. The whole Mormon church thinks we're apostates. They don't know it's themselves that are tipping on the lips of hell. They don't know we have the Spirit right here in these canyons. I see it clear now why God put your father in Ezra's way. Isn't it the truth that you can't outguess God? He sent you to us so you can save your folks. That's your mission, Arabella Gurney. You're going to save your father and mother and your brothers and sisters.''

After supper Arabella went to her room. For a while she resisted sleep; lying on the bed, still wearing the yellow dress, she tried to think about what she must do. She wondered if she should let herself sleep for a while, then rise, put on her jeans and boots, and escape through the window. She estimated that the highway was nine or ten miles south of Reuben's village and that the dig lay east not more than twenty or twenty-five miles in a straight line across the canyons. As she grew more drowsy, images of Winifred and Reuben and of her father and mother flickered in her mind. It seemed that she must go home, just as her father and mother had constantly asked her to do in their letters. When the summer's work was over at the dig, she must go home and try again. It would be a terrible thing, because she would have to tell what had happened between her and Franklin. Inevitably there would be a temporary excommunication before she could fit back properly into the church, and who knew how long it might be before God would forgive her? As she went off into sleep, Arabella was wondering again how she could ever learn to stifle her warped, perverted ego.

A loud knock roused her from her sleep. ''How come you to lock this door?'' Reuben said as she opened it. ''Nobody here is going to rob or murder you.''

Reuben bent, peered under the bed, and pulled out Arabella's boots, jeans, halter, and the necklace made from the Tabegauche point. ''Winifred told me you wouldn't let her haul these away. Those aren't any clothes fit for a woman.'' He stood and kicked the clothes into their former place under the bed. ''Tomorrow you burn them. Winifred will show you the barrel where we burn trash.'' In his hand Reuben held the Tabegauche point. He took out a pocket knife and cut off the nylon cord, then threw the cord into a corner and put the point into his shirt pocket.

Reuben sat by Arabella on the edge of the bed. ''Maybe it's time for you and me to have a little talk. I just as well tell you where I have been all afternoon. I have been in the junipers wrestling with God. He told me you were to be destroyed. I said, I can't do it, she's too young, she doesn't have any better sense, give her another chance. When I came out of the junipers, I was so low a horse could have walked on me. Then I met Ezra and he told me about meeting your father. Just like that! It was a sign. I saw all at once what God had in mind. He's put a condition on you, Arabella. If you'll repent and do your duty, if you'll save your father and mother and bring them to the true church, he'll forgive you. More than that, he put it in my heart tonight that you'll be the mother of a great man. I couldn't tell it in front of all the others how great he will be, but I'm going to tell you. One of your babies is going to be the prophet of this church someday.''

Arabella was weeping silently.

"But you have to come clean now. I know you have been sleeping with that curly-headed fellow regular. Were there any others?''

"No. Just him.''

"How come you never quit when I told you to?''

"I didn't even start till then.''

"How come?''

"Because I hate God.''

Reuben got up, went to the window, and peered out into the night. With his back to Arabella he said, "I never heard anyone say that before in my whole life.'' He turned around. "But I guess it had to come out.''

"Help me,'' Arabella said. Her final reserve had vanished. It suddenly seemed that Reuben's heretical ideas were true, that by the merest accident she had been led to the authentic order of God, hidden from other eyes in these hot, remote canyons. Swept by a need to confess, she told Reuben how her anger had appeared, how it had emerged little by little over the years until, in recent times, it had loomed like an impassable wall. She told him how a perverse freedom had become the most precious thing of her life, how in her burning, vital center she had wished to confront God, to invite damnation, to perform irrevocable acts against Him. "But I want to kill all that,'' she said, sobbing passionately. "I want to cut it out of me, to bury it. I want to be obedient, to follow the commandments. I just want peace."

Reuben's face had lost its relentless severity. "It will be a long, hard pull for you," he said. "Satan has worked on you. The reason is you're one of God's choicest spirits. Did you know that? Satan threw everything he had at you. It's no wonder you've done the things you did."

He shifted, looked around the room, pulled out his watch. "You'll be all right now. You're among the proper people. But we don't have to say everything tonight. There's time enough for talk tomorrow." He pulled down the counterpane and began to unbutton his shirt.

"You don't mean to sleep here, do you?" she burst out. "I couldn't do that. We aren't married."

He stared at her. "Who would marry us? I'm the prophet." He left the room for a moment and returned carrying two books. One was a large Bible bound in black leather. "Look," he said, "I wrote it right here on the first day I ever saw you: *Arabella Gurney, ninth wife unto Reuben Millring*. Right then we were married."

"I can't do it," she blurted.

Reuben's face tightened with angry perplexity. "Do you think a man *wants* wives? When God commanded me to take Theresa into the Covenant, I argued with him. I said, I already have four wives and she is married to another man, though I admit he was a son of perdition. I said, It doesn't make sense, but God struck me with fear. You don't quibble with the Almighty."

He sat again on the edge of the bed. "It's easy to think it is Reuben Millring that wants this, but it isn't me you're backing out on." He set the Bible on the bed and opened the other book, which was a copy of the Doctrine and Covenants. He leaned over the pages of the book. "Emma Smith didn't like it when the Prophet Joseph took more wives. She stood up to the Prophet; she wasn't going to pay him any mind. But God warned her. Listen to this: *But if she will not abide this commandment she shall be destroyed, saith the Lord; for I am the Lord, thy God, and will destroy her if she abide not my law.*"

He closed the book and spoke in a hushed voice. "Have you ever seen an angel of destruction? I have seen them. I don't want to see any more. One night I looked out the window; I saw a fire on the ridge. I knew it couldn't be a fire. I didn't want to go, but I knew I had to. I saddled the mare, and when I got there, I saw a vision. It was Armageddon. There were fires and earthquakes; buildings fell in; people screamed and there wasn't anybody to help them; pet dogs went crazy, they tore up their masters and the little kids who used to play with them; snakes came out of the ground and strangled the wicked."

Tears tracked Arabella's face. She stood and unbuttoned the dress. She stepped out of it, pulled slip straps off her shoulders, and let the slip fall to the floor. She got onto the bed and waited with tightly shut eyes to receive Reuben. She crowded back her protest, shoved it roughly into a darkened chamber of her mind, slammed a door shut on it. She concentrated upon a single hope; she applied energy to it, willed it fervently, forced it into thoughts and images. She hoped that the shocks and bruises, the indignities and terrors she had suffered during this long day were the fire of God's furnace. She hoped that, when this night was through, a new Arabella would arise, purged of her perversity. She felt, hot upon her face, the gusts of Reuben's passionate breath. As clearly as if her eyes were open and she watched in the light of day, she saw the deep seams in his cheeks, the furrows in his brow, the bristling grey of his hair, his steel-rimmed eyes. All her life she had known him. From the talk of teachers, friends, and parents, from the word of the Scriptures, she had assembled his portrait. In Reuben's face—aflame with conviction, wrathful against sin, touched by the promise of a remote salvation—Arabella saw the face of God.

Near dawn, Arabella awoke from a fitful, feverish sleep. She was shaken by her terrible dreams. In one, she had lain upon an operating table, her bared belly swollen to giant proportions. A zipper ran from her navel down through the crevice of her pudendum and buttocks, anchoring at the base of her spinal column. A doctor seized the handle and unzipped her, pulling the flaps of her belly apart and peering within. An eruption of wadded papers, shooting up like a geyser, broke past the doctor's face and spilled out upon the floor.

Arabella leaned over the side of the table and watched as the wads squirmed and writhed and stretched themselves into smooth sheets of newsprint. She saw headlines in bold black letters: *Welcome to Sunday Worship of the Ever Changing; Sipapu Raped, Left for Dead; President Orders Change of Oil for the Living Engine.* In another dream Arabella sat at the kitchen table with her mother, who shelled peas close beside her. Cookies and milk were on the table. On the floor, between the table and the cookstove, was a deep tub filled with shimmering, blackened blood. Something stirred in it—perhaps the iridescent protrusions of afterbirth, or perhaps nothing more than the backs of swimming fish. Arabella put her hand over her mouth, suppressing a cry. Her mother looked on calmly, opening pods one after another and spilling the peas into a pan in her lap. "I didn't know it would be so bloody," Arabella said. "It usually isn't this bad," her mother replied blandly.

Reuben sighed, spoke an unintelligible word, and turned in the bed. A terrible revulsion for this strange, imperious man came over Arabella. She slid from the bed and crouched on the floor. The events of the previous day crowded freshly upon her. Squatting nude and defenseless, she became filled with rage. She saw that she had been treated with consummate indignity, that she had been violated beyond all measure. She groped beneath the bed, pulled out her jeans, boots, and halter and put them on. Looking up as she tied her bootlaces, she saw that Reuben stood at the foot of the bed.

"Take those clothes off," he said quietly.

Arabella sprinted for the door, but before she could grasp the knob Reuben lunged for her, seized her arm, and flung her spinning across the room. She crashed into the dresser and fell to the floor. Reuben knelt by her side and gripped her shoulder, digging his fingers into her flesh. "This is your last chance," he said. He rose and put on his shirt and pants. "Breakfast will be ready pretty soon," he went on. "Get out of those clothes and put on that dress. Then come on out to the kitchen." He sat on the edge of the bed and tied his shoes.

Arabella stood and supported herself at the dresser. She looked at the heavy porcelain pitcher and basin. She lifted the basin quietly and turned suddenly. Before Reuben could stand, she brought its edge down with all her force upon his head. Reuben sprawled across the floor; thick blood flowed from the split in his skull. With her hand clapped over her gaping mouth and her eyes wide with horror, Arabella approached him. Slowly, rigidly, she bent, tugged his body over, reached into his shirt pocket, and pulled out the Tabegauche point. She looked at it for a moment; then, clutching it so tightly that it cut her fingers, she fled the room.

She ran through the village and over the eastern ridge. Before her lay a chopped, fissured land illuminated by the rising sun. Far to the northeast were the blue Abajo mountains. Without hesitation, she went on, slipping and sliding down slopes, crossing canyon bottoms, pulling herself through thickets of willow and ash, scrambling up ridges, scaling minor cliffs. At intervals she rested, standing with heaving ribs and gasping until she could summon new energy to plunge forward once more. At noon, she found herself in the bottom of a deep gorge. She discovered a small pothole of tepid water and drank deeply, then followed the gorge downward. It sank between high vertical walls, its course ruptured by chutes and falls and masses of tumbled rock over which she laboriously pulled herself. The sun's rays beat directly upon her; the bare rock of the gorge radiated a baking heat. At midafternoon she stood at the edge of an immense plunge and knew that she could not make her way south to the highway as she had hoped. She retraced her steps, found the pothole, drank again, and continued along the upward course of the gorge. By evening she had found a breach in its wall and had clambered out onto a high eastward ridge.

The Abajos remained as blue and remote as they had seemed that morning. Southeastward, in the dim distance of the twilight, were a mesa and a sail-like pinnacle which Arabella recognized. Her spirits fell. She knew she would not reach the dig the next day; cutting across country, she would be until the day after or even the day after that. She was thirsty and throbbing with fatigue. In an outcropping of rock she found a crevice cushioned by soil and grass. She settled into it as the dusk grew. Bright stars emerged one by one. A faint fluorescent glow filled the great arch of the sky; she scanned it with impatient eyes, as if she hoped to find among the imaginary lines of the familiar constellations some friend or a sign of comfort. She found the Dippers and Polaris, and then she found Cygnus the Swan, just risen above the eastern horizon. She stared at its glimmering, winking stars. A dreadful thought came to her: Cygnus was a clock for reading the progress of the night; it would have to rise, pass overhead, and descend low into the western sky before morning would come.

A horror prowled at the edge of her consciousness. She could no longer resist the memory of Reuben's sprawling body, his cloven skull, the thick pudding of blood which had run out upon the bedroom floor. Throughout the day she had preserved herself by detachment. She had dug a moat between herself and the killing. It was as if she had viewed it from a distance, not even sure that the bludgeoning had occurred; it was as if some dark, unknown person had emerged from thin air to strike Reuben down with vengeful satisfaction. But she knew it had been none other than herself. She would have to tell everything to the sheriff, to the county attorney, to Dr. Muhlestein, to her poor father and mother. And what could she say to Franklin? All day she had doggedly carried the Tabegauche point, until now her hands were chafed and sore from its sharp edges. The point had seemed inordinately precious, a token of hope, a sign that Franklin might still love her. But now she doubted. There was a devastating absurdity about her vacillations of mind, a monstrous risibility about her having agreed to let Reuben make love to her.

Another, greater horror came over Arabella. God was dead. He did not exist. He was a mere fantasy, a domestication by which the human mind attempted to shelter itself against the terror of annihilation. She had seen that fact, if only she had had the courage to admit it, in the moment of retrieving the Tabegauche point from Reuben's pocket. Irresistibly, against all Christian logic and tradition, Reuben's inert, extinguished body persuaded her. Her hands, clasping his shoulder as she pulled his body over, conveyed the message. The dimensions of death flowed through her fingers. Death was forever.

She shifted her position in the crevice, listened to the whir of a nighthawk overhead, and looked again at the brilliant, burning stars. Her emotions were a flash flood in a desert wash, a rumbling wall of muddy spume and rolling rocks. Hysterically, Arabella acknowledged the mortal kindred to which she belonged. She was a molecule of stone; she was a corpuscle of blood in the arteries of the nighthawk overhead. Her body was a machine, a transport and shell for its genes, those desperate perpetuators of the fever of life which, from their beginning in the primordial soup, had accepted without protest the senseless round of competition, replication, and death. Her spirit was chemical; love and compassion, justice, reverence, courage, and despair were mere exhalations of earth, air, fire, and water. Everywhere the millstones of the universe degraded compounds and elements into finer powder, or, quixotically reversing, elevated them into greater complexity. In all things, at all times, was flux. Reuben Millring was dead, and Arabella did not know what had become of him.

She waited for morning, forcing her eyes away from Cygnus the Swan, grimly instructing herself that she must ignore the passage of time. It seemed that she waited for an enormous period—for longer than an hour, longer than two. When she opened her eyes and looked for Cygnus, her despair deepened. The constellation had scarcely moved. Time wore on. It seemed that she had looked a hundred times to see if Cygnus had advanced an inch. Then, when she did not expect it, when she had not even recognized that she had become drowsy, she slept. She awoke strangely refreshed and looked for Cygnus but could not find it. She looked more widely, and there, far in the western sky, stood the Swan. Exhilaration seized her. She rose from the crevice and saw the faintest glow of dawn upon the eastern horizon. Deep gratitude came over her for the propitious sleep; it seemed to be a palpable gift, an undreamed-of treasure. Far away a coyote howled—steep, shrill, utterly clear. Explosions of high, brittle sound raced across the miles as coyote after coyote relayed the song. The chorus fell away in a cacophony of barking, yipping, and howling. Arabella stood, forgetful of her thirst, her stiffened body, and the chill of the desert dawn, taken by wonder in the subtle advance of light. Close at hand rocks, trees, and bending grass emerged into the clarity of day; then in the distance appeared ridges, buttes, and peaks. An orange fire flared along the horizon; a bright rim of incandescent cloud burned in the eastern sky.

Arabella was immeasurably relieved. Looking at a berry-laden juniper and a tall-stemmed yucca, she could almost believe they were friends who regarded her with warm affection. The wilderness bore her no grudge, was still willing to bless her. She was alive, and the universe was holy. She would mourn for Reuben, who was dead, and for all the others who could not bear to know of their ultimate extinction. As for herself, she had decided to be courageous. In the open palm of her hand the Tabeguache point mirrored the rising sun. Anxious to cover ground while the day was cool, she strode to the edge of the ridge to take her bearings. An ephemeral predator upon a minor planet, she went forward free and filled with grace.